ALWAYS

A ROSEWOOD NOVELLA

SHAW HART

*

We started as friends.

Evangeline "Evan" Rauley is a small-town girl. She was born and raised in Rosewood, Colorado, and while both of her friends left to go to college, she never had that luxury.

She was raised by her mother and living on a single-parent salary was never easy. She's been working the odd job since she was fifteen, saving up until she can finally afford to open her own nursery.

Things are going smoothly until one day a blast from the past arrives back in town.

Jasper "Mack" Mackelroy.

He was Evangeline's childhood crush, her friend, the guy who has fueled every one of her fantasies.

He was also the town bad boy.

Everyone always warned her to stay away from him, that he was nothing but trouble, but she never could resist the pull between them.

It looks like some things never change....

ONE

Jasper

IT DOESN'T LOOK like anything has changed in Rosewood and that's saying a lot considering that I've been gone for close to a decade. I had thought that I would never come back, especially when my younger brother, Gray, moved away, but then I got the call and here I am.

Leave it to my father to ruin all of my plans.

I drive down First Street, stopping at one of the three stoplights in town and drumming the fingers of my non-injured hand on the steering wheel. My arm and shoulder are killing me and I can't wait to get to the hotel, take some pain pills and crash for the night.

I spot Mrs. Merkle slowly walking down the sidewalk, her cane tap-tapping with each step. She was my third-grade teacher and was one of the only adults to ever try to help me. She's smiling, enjoying the cool night air and I watch her head into The Little Moo ice cream parlor.

Seeing her has me feeling confused about this place and

I hate it. I hate Rosewood, but there were a few bright spots. It just sucks that it would be easier for me if I just forgot about those spots.

The light turns green and I take a left onto Main Street, cruising past the shops that I could never afford to go to when I was younger.

Most people would probably be nostalgic about being back home, but this town doesn't have many good memories in it for me. There aren't many places that I can drive by or see that has me flashing back to a fond memory.

My mom left when I was young, escaping from my asshole father. Unfortunately for Gray and me, she didn't take us with her. I can barely remember her, so maybe my life would have sucked just as much with her as it did with my dad.

I take another left and notice a sign that I don't remember. The Garden Goddess. It looks like a greenhouse or plant nursery. I slow down, taking in all of the flowers and the little log cabin building. There's a huge greenhouse behind it and a sign that says the grand opening will be held next weekend.

I guess that explains why I don't remember the place.

I'm about to take a right and head toward my hotel when I spot a familiar raven-haired woman.

I almost swerve off of the road trying to get a closer look. Could it really be her? I would have thought that she left town after high school and I wonder why she's still in town.

I slow down, my eyes greedily taking in the curvy woman that I remember from my youth.

Evangeline Rauley.

She was the girl of my dreams. I take in the differences from the last time that I saw her. Her hair is longer, her waist curvier, but she's still got this pull to her, this energy, that has always drawn me in.

Maybe it's the way that she holds herself or maybe it's just who she is. Either way, I was crazy about her growing up but I didn't have much to offer anyone back then. She was way out of my league. Besides, I wasn't in a position to start a relationship. I was barely keeping my head above water as is.

She bends down, fussing with some flowers there, a soft smile on her face. Evangeline was always so sweet. Everyone else in town used to see me as the town bad boy because I couldn't go a week without getting a new bruise. I never knew if they really didn't know that the bruises were from my father or if they did know and just didn't care enough to look into it.

I want to stay, to study her for hours but I force myself to turn and drive the two blocks over to my hotel. I'm still not in a great position to offer her a relationship or much of anything.

I climb out of the rental car, dropping my hoodie over the bandages on my arm as I grab my bags from the trunk. I debate if I should grab the sling from the back seat where I threw it, but I hate wearing that thing, so I leave it there.

It doesn't take me long to check in. No one really visits Rosewood. It's a little bit too much of a drive from Denver or Colorado Springs and so we really only get the occasional tourist or person passing through.

My room is on the third floor and I take the elevator, dragging my big green military bags with me. I open the door, taking in the worn carpet, single queen-sized bed with the ugly comforter, and the TV that looks like it's from the eighties.

The AC sputters to life and I sigh. I need to get the hell out of this town as fast as I can.

I groan as I sit down on the bed. My arm is killing me, and I know that now that I'm here for the night, I should take some more pain pills. I fish them out of my bag and wonder if Gray is on his way down here yet.

My brother works as a tattoo artist at some renowned shop up in Pittsburgh and his hours are all over the place. I never know when he's going to have time to talk to me or when he's with a client. We used to be closer when we were kids, but when I left for the military, we drifted apart.

I always used to wonder if my dad was telling him lies about me after I left or if he was just angry with me for leaving to deal with our dad alone, even if I only did it to keep a roof over our heads and food on the table.

I lay back, closing my eyes and replay the message in my head of when I told my brother that our father was dead.

"Hey, what's up?" he asks after the call connects.

"Hey, Gray," I say. I sound exhausted even to my own ears.

"Hey, are you back in the states?"

I haven't told him that I was injured yet and that I can't go back to the military or that I spent the last three weeks at a hospital in Germany getting stitched back up.

"No, but I'm headed back now. I, uh, I got some news today," I start.

"Yeah?" he asks and I can hear the nerves in his voice.

He sounds like that kid that I left behind all those years ago.

"It's Dad, Gray," I sigh.

"What about him?" he asks, his voice hard.

"He's dead," I reply, my tone flat, unfeeling.

"What?"

"They think it was a heart attack. Honestly, I'm surprised that his liver didn't give out on him. The funeral is going to be this weekend. I'm headed home to plan it now. I didn't think that you would want to be there for the planning part..." I say, trailing off when Gray hasn't made a sound.

"I can if you need me to," he offers, but I can hear the reluctance in his voice.

I don't blame him. I don't want to deal with them or anything else with our dad either, but I've always been the one to do the hard things. Duties of being a big brother, I guess.

"No, Gray. It's okay, I can take care of it."

"Thanks, Jasp. Let me know if you need anything before this weekend."

"Will do. Do you want me to pay for your ticket home?" I offer.

"No, Nora might come with me, so I'll get my ticket... but thank you."

He clears his throat and we both stay on the phone.

"I'll see you and Nora this weekend," I say finally.

"See you."

I stand, my skin feeling too tight as I think about every-thing that needs to be done. I don't want to stay here. I don't want to be in this town or dealing with any of this.

I grab my keys and head back downstairs. It's still light out as I climb behind the wheel, driving around town, trying to calm down.

It feels like everything in my life is falling down around me and I'm angry.

I'm out of the military now that I've been injured. Medically discharged but I've done that job for so long that I have no idea what I want to do with my life next.

I have no car, no home, nothing.

I can't help but think about the day that I enlisted. I had been searching for a job in town for months, but nothing paid enough or had benefits. My dad was always drunk and he disappeared every payday with our money.

I was at the end of my rope and so I enlisted. I hated having to grow up so fast, hated worrying about Gray back home and if he was alright, but it was the only option that I saw. It was either I joined the military or we lived on the streets. I could have called CPS but they would have removed Gray and taken him to a new town. I couldn't do that to him. He's been in love with his best friend, Nora, since the day that he saw her and I didn't want them to be separated.

I find myself driving down my old street and parking in front of what used to be our house. It was never much to look at and things have only gotten worse in the ten years since I've been gone.

The roof is sagging and I think that there might actually even be a hole in one spot. The porch steps are just as bad and don't look like they could support anyone's weight. The whole front looks dirty and I can't imagine the sides of the house or back are much better.

Overgrown grass and weeds are starting to grow over the walkway and side of the house and I groan just thinking about how much work it's going to be to get rid of this place. I'm not sure that it can be saved. It looks like it should be condemned.

This house is the only thing that my father owns, and it's not surprising that he let it go to hell. He was never great at caring for anything besides himself.

Part of me had hoped that maybe I could stay here but even if I was mentally able to put up with all of the terrible memories inside of the house, I doubt that it's physically safe to stay here.

I guess that I'll be staying in the hotel after all and this doesn't look like it will be the quick trip home that I was hoping it would be.

"Dammit," I sigh as I take one last look at the house and climb back behind the wheel.

TWO

Evangeline

"DON'T FORGET the Zebra Cakes and the popcorn!" my mom calls to me as I head out to do some grocery shopping.

"Got it!" I call back.

I can barely hear her over the sound of *Wheel of Fortune* blaring over the TV speakers. She calls out an answer as the door closes behind me and I can hear her clapping when she gets it right.

My mom is quite the character. She raised me as a single mom and has always been the outspoken one. She was the mom who knitted me sweaters and accidentally signed us up for pole dancing classes when I was sixteen. She had meant to do Zumba and I'm still not sure how she managed to mix those two up. The classes had been fun though.

I'm happier in my garden, soil under my nails and a giant sun hat covering my pale skin. That doesn't stop my mom from always trying to push me out of my comfort zone though.

There was the blind date the other month that never actually happened since the guy stood me up. I didn't even know that it was a date. I thought that I was just meeting my mom for dinner and when she never showed up, I had driven home in a panic only to see her in her recliner, happily watching her shows. It was only then that she admitted that she had set me up with someone. She was furious that he hadn't shown up but I think that I dodged a bullet.

She's always pushing me to meet new people, especially men, but I'm beginning to think that maybe dating and settling down like that just isn't for me.

I hop into my truck, smiling when I see The Garden Goddess logo on the side. I'm getting ready to open my nursery and flower shop next week and I'm so excited. I've been working toward this dream for years and it's finally about to come true.

I head down our long driveway and into town. We live close to the edge of Rosewood and it's going to take me close to ten minutes to get to the grocery store.

Rosewood isn't that big and it only takes about twenty minutes to get from one side to the other. It's the kind of town where everyone knows everyone else and all of their dirty little secrets.

I wave at a few people, slowing and pulling over to the curb when I see my childhood friend, Sydney, outside of her new apartment.

She just moved back to town a few days ago and it's been great having her back in town. She's still getting settled and we haven't had much time to catch up yet but I'm hoping to fix that soon.

"Hey, Syd!" I call and she looks up, pushing her mane of dark brown hair out of her face.

"Evan!" she says, coming over to the side of my truck.

"Where are you off to?"

"I'm out job hunting. It doesn't look like there are that many places hiring," she says with a sigh.

Her green eyes dim and I know that she's getting nervous that she hasn't been able to find anything. I'm sure that she has student loan payments that need to be paid and she lives with her grandma who raised her.

"I'm sure that you'll find something soon! I'll keep my eye out for you and maybe The Garden Goddess will take off and I can hire you," I say with a grin.

"I'm rooting for you! Do you need any help getting stuff set up?"

Sydney studied interior design at college and I know that she's going to have a hard time finding something in that field in this town.

"Want to come see how I set it up? Maybe give me some pointers?"

"Sure! I'll stop by later today?"

"Perfect. I'm just running to the store to grab some groceries. I'll grab us lunch after I drop that off and meet you at the nursery?"

"Sounds good. I meant to text you. I ran into Rowan and she was asking about setting up a girl's night soon."

"Yeah, I wanted to set one up too. I'll start a group chat later," I promise and she smiles and waves at me as we say goodbye and head down the road to the store.

I park in the lot of the Rosewood Market and head inside, grabbing a cart and pulling up my list as I go. I grab some fruit and vegetables, debate over the chip aisle, and make my way over to the frozen pizza.

I gasp as my cart rams into someone else's and I look up to see a blast from my past.

"No bruises," I mumble as I take in Jasper's perfect face.

I had the biggest crush on him when I was younger and I always thought that I would grow out of being into bad boys.

That's what Jasper was. The town bad boy. I remember that people used to say that he would be dead or in prison by the time that he turned twenty-five.

Although, I never really understood that. He was always quiet and kind in school. He never bullied anyone, never acted out in class, nothing.

The only thing that gave people the impression that Jasper was a troublemaker were the bruises.

There wasn't a week that went by where Jasper wasn't sporting at least one new bruise. I used to wonder who he was fighting but we never got quite close enough for me to feel comfortable asking. I think that everyone in town was shocked when he enlisted right after high school and never came back.

"What was that?" Jasper asks, his grayish-blue eyes studying my face like he's trying to memorize every detail.

"Nothing! Welcome home," I say, trying not to grimace at almost being caught.

"Uh, thanks."

"When did you get back?" I ask as we both move our carts out of the way of Mrs. Shamton.

"Just last night."

"What brings you back?" I ask, my eyes noticing the scars and his neck and chin and the white bandages on his left arm for the first time. He's got a five o'clock shadow that is partially covering them and I didn't see them at first. "Oh my gosh! Are you alright?"

I reach out, trying to do I don't know what, but I pull my hand back before I can touch him.

"Yeah, I'm fine. The bandage just makes it look bad," he says with a shrug but I can see him wincing and I know that it must still hurt.

I wonder what happened, but just like when we were kids, I don't feel close enough to ask him.

"Are you on leave?" I ask.

I know that he was in the military. Last I heard, he was overseas fighting.

"No, I was medically discharged so I'm out."

"So, you moved back home then?"

"No, my father passed away. I'm here for the funeral and to sell his house."

"Oh, I'm so sorry. I had no idea."

"It's alright. It wasn't really any great loss."

His words catch me off guard but I sidestep them.

"I haven't seen your dad in town in a while."

"Yeah, I'm sure that he's frequenting places that you have no business being," he mumbles, his face darkening as he talks about his father.

"Well, it's still nice to have you back."

"Thanks. I saw your nursery last night when I got to town. It looks good."

"Thanks! I'm so excited for the opening. You should come. We're going to do a raffle and have some food and drinks."

"I'll have to stop by," he says with a small smile.

That was the thing about Jasper. He never really smiled or showed other emotions. It was just those grayish-blue eyes taking everything in.

My phone goes off and it's my mom's ringtone.

"I should get that," I say apologetically.

"No worries. It was nice seeing you again. We'll have to grab dinner and catch up some more soon," he says as he starts to push his cart past me.

I can only stare after him as I wonder just what exactly he meant by that.

Did Jasper Mackelroy just ask me out?

THREE

Jasper

I'M STANDING outside the hotel the next day, my neck feeling hot as I look around Rosewood. I can feel people staring at me, and I don't like it. This place never felt like home and I feel even more alienated now that I'm back.

I'm in the shadows in the little nook by the front door people watching. It's a slow day, only a few people out and about.

My eyes lock on Evangeline as she walks down the sidewalk on the other side of the road. Her round hips sway with each step and my mouth starts to water. I want to run my hands over those curves. I want to explore every inch of her.

I shift, my eyes locked on Evangeline as she heads past my hiding spot. She's wearing a pair of jeans with dirt on the knees and I can picture her doing other things on her knees.

I get lost in my daydreams and maybe that's why I don't notice when my brother pulls into the parking lot.

Gray and Nora park in the spot next to my rental car and I push off from the hotel wall and head over to greet them. It's weird, but I'm nervous to see my brother again. I've been shot, blown up, fought in wars, but the thought of facing my brother has me feeling anxious.

I take one last look at Evangeline before she turns the corner and heads toward her nursery.

"What the fuck?" Gray growls, stalking the few feet over to me with a scowl on his face, his eyes locked on my bandaged arm and then the scars on my neck. "You're hurt?"

"Yeah," I say, my hand rubbing at the back of my neck. "My unit got hit on our last mission. I was going to tell you but then I got the call about Dad."

"And you just decided to let me know when I saw you?" Gray asks and I can tell that he's annoyed with me for hiding this.

"We're just glad that you're alright," Nora says, laying her hand on Gray's arm. "It's good to see you again, Jasper. I'm sorry for your loss."

Those last words don't ring true and I know that no one who ever knew him really thinks that Rod Mackelroy's death is any real loss.

"Thanks, Nora. It's good to see you too. Are you guys all checked in?"

"Not yet. We're headed in now."

I nod, following after Gray and Nora as we all head for the hotel lobby. Gray heads over to check in and Nora stays with me off to the side.

"Do you need me to do anything for tomorrow?" she

asks, careful not to let Gray hear her, and I wonder how my brother is taking the news.

"No, I already made all of the plans. I don't anticipate it being a big funeral. Rod wasn't exactly a pillar of the community."

Nora gives me a sad smile and I wonder if she's thinking about her own father and home life. She didn't exactly have it better than we did.

"It starts at ten, right?" she asks and I nod.

"Yeah, then I thought we could grab lunch downtown somewhere. I need to go over to the house and clean it out sometime this week too."

"Are you sure that you should be doing that?" she asks, nodding toward my injured side.

"I'll be fine," I promise.

"When do you go back to the Army?" Gray asks as he joins us.

"I don't. I was medically discharged."

"So, what are you going to do?"

"I thought I'd stay in Rosewood for a little bit. I need to clean up the house and take care of a few more things."

"Then what?" Gray asks with a frown.

"Honestly, I don't know. I think I might like trying to figure that part out though."

My mind flashes back to the sway of Evangeline's hips and my dirty fantasies.

"We're on the fourth floor," Gray tells us and I nod.

"I'm the third," I say as he hits the button for the elevator. "Room 314, if you need anything."

Gray just nods, and Nora leans against him, her eyes starting to droop.

"See you in the morning," I say as we get to my floor and they both nod sleepily.

I head to my room but I can't seem to fall asleep. I try pacing around the room, taking a shower, watching TV. Nothing works.

I stare at the ceiling, letting my mind go back to thoughts of Evangeline. I must doze off because I wake the next morning only remembering images of Evangeline spread out on a bed, flowers all around her, and that sweet smile on her face.

I groan, rolling over and climb out of bed. I want to go back to sleep and my dreams of Evangeline whispering dirty things in my ear but then I remember what today is and my mood plummets.

"Shit," I say as I throw my legs over the side of the bed, dragging my hands down my face.

I shower and pull on the only suit that I own. I need to check in with the church and priest and make sure that everything is set. I should check with Gray and Nora and see if they want to ride together.

I take one last look around the hotel room before I grab my phone and call Gray. He answers, sounding groggy and I wonder if I woke him up.

"Hey, I was just calling to ask if you and Nora wanted to ride together today?"

"Yeah, that works. Nora is just getting out of the shower now, so we'll be ready in twenty."

"Sounds good. I'll go grab us some coffee and food and meet you in the lobby then."

"Thanks," he says and we both hang up.

I wish that we could have deeper conversations. Every time we talk lately it feels like we never really say anything. I know that this is at least partly my fault. I'm the one who left and my job made it so that I couldn't talk often or about what I was doing half of the time. I wonder if it's too late for me to make this right.

We eat breakfast and Gray drives us all to the funeral in silence. I'm not sure if they're still tired from their late flight or if the funeral is throwing everyone off.

We head into the church and I'm not surprised to see that it's just the three of us here. Gray heads up to pay his respects and say goodbye and I take a seat in one of the pews. I've already seen him and I don't need to say anything else to the bastard.

Nora and Gray join me in the pew and the preacher starts his sermon a few minutes later. It's a little awkward to sit there and listen to the preacher go on and on about our dad being in a better place and walking with Jesus now. It feels like one of us should speak up and inform the preacher that there's no way in hell our dad made it into Heaven.

Gray and I exchange a look and I can tell that we're both thinking the same thing. I smile, holding in a laugh as I relax in the pew.

The funeral doesn't last long and soon we're filing back out to Gray's car and following the hearse over to the cemetery and standing around his casket.

We form a small circle around the grave and watch in silence as the priest says a quick prayer as he's lowered into the ground. None of us thought to bring flowers and his headstone seems bare next to the big ones on either side of him.

"Did you want a minute?" I ask, nodding toward the casket in the ground and Gray shakes his head.

"Do you?"

"No."

Just like that, the funeral is over.

We head back to Gray's car and all slide in.

"I need to go by the house. See how bad it is," I say as I tug at my tie.

"We'll go with you, but maybe we should change first," Nora suggests.

We pile back into the rental car and drive back across town to the hotel. It's still just as dead as it was when we got here last night.

"Meet back down here in twenty?" I ask as we ride up to my floor.

"Sounds good."

I change quickly, grateful to be out of the suit and tie. It doesn't take me long to get ready and I send a message to Gray, asking them if they're hungry and where they want to go for lunch. Gray texts back suggesting that we just grab Wendy's or something. I send back a thumbs up and grab my car keys.

The house looks just as bad in broad daylight as it did the other night and my fingers tighten on the steering wheel as I park the car.

No one moves and I can tell that none of us are happy to be here and that no one wants to go inside.

Nora's old house is just down the street and I catch her looking over at it, a thin layer of fear clouding her eyes.

Her dad was an alcoholic just like mine, but as far as I know, he never hit her. I'm sure that her brother, Niall, would have killed him if he had. Hell, I would have helped him if he had asked. Nora and Gray getting together is inevitable, so I've always thought of her as a little sister. She's family.

Gray says something to Nora, calming her down and getting her to look away from her childhood home. I climb out, wanting to give them some privacy.

They follow me up to the front door and Gray grabs

Nora's hand as we maneuver our way around the sagging porch.

"We'll have to fix that if we want to sell this place," I mumble and I can't help but glare around the house.

There isn't much left. I'm sure that Rod has sold or pawned everything of value over the years. Gray is rooted to the spot, his eyes darting around the place and I wonder which memories have him. Nothing good ever happened here.

"Where should we start?" Gray asks, looking over to me.

"I'm not sure there's much to do. I was expecting way worse but there isn't much left. I'll have to hire a crew or do an inspection to see if we need to fix it up or start from scratch and then we can list the place."

"Do you want to look around? See if there's anything that you want?" Nora asks and we both shake their heads no immediately.

"I haven't needed anything here for the last five years so I can live without it now. Let's just go," Gray says and we all nod, letting him lead the way back down the front porch steps and over to the car.

This town doesn't hold good memories for any of us. It's why we all were so desperate to escape it when we were younger.

We pass by The Garden Goddess and I wonder if maybe it's about time that I changed that.

"Can you pull over here?" I ask from the back seat and Gray nods, turning into the nursery parking lot.

"Doing some gardening?" Gray asks dryly and I just roll my eyes.

"We're going to need to fix up the outside to sell the house. I just want to see if they do landscaping. I'll be right back."

I climb out of the car and make my way over to where Evangeline is busy setting up a stand of some kind of tall grass.

"Hey," I say, clearing my throat and she spins around to face me.

"Hey, enjoying the sunshine?" she asks with a smile and I'm about to lie and say yes, but I can't.

"Uh, actually we just buried my dad."

"Oh my gosh! I'm so sorry. I didn't realize that the funeral is today."

Her face is bright red and I didn't mean to embarrass her. I just didn't want to lie to her.

"It's okay. He wasn't much of a dad. I actually wanted to see if you did landscaping? I need to fix up my dad's house and sell it."

"I don't officially, but I would love to help you with some ideas," she says with that sweet smile of hers.

"That would be great. Thanks, Evangeline," I say honestly.

"Of course," she says and I want to ask her out but it doesn't seem like the right time.

"I'll talk to you later," I promise and she nods as I turn and head back toward the car.

I climb in and we drive the remaining blocks back to the hotel in silence.

"What time are you leaving in the morning?" I ask.

"Eight," Gray says.

I can see him staring at me in the reflection on the elevator doors and I try not to shift. He's watching me like I'm a puzzle and he can't figure out how to solve me.

"Did you want to grab dinner tonight?" Gray asks as we stop on my floor.

I want to say yes and spend more time with my brother

but my arm is killing me and I have an appointment at the VA to go over the latest x-rays.

"I need to make a few calls and then I have a doctor appointment in Denver in two hours. It was good seeing you both though."

"You too," Nora says, hugging me goodbye before she steps to the side so that Gray and I can talk.

"I'll talk to you soon. Let me know if you need any more help with the house or if you need anything else. Let me know how the doctor appointment goes," Gray says, his voice thick with emotion.

I know that today has been hard for him. Being back here is hard for all of us.

"I will. See you guys."

With that, the elevator doors close and I head back to my room alone. I make a call to an inspection company and arrange for them to come check out the house tomorrow. Then it's time for me to head over to Denver for my appointment.

I rub my shoulder as I sit and wait to be called back. It doesn't take long and as soon as the doctor comes in, I know that it's probably not great news.

"So, it's still inflamed and I don't love the way that the bone is mending," he says as he flips through my file.

"So, I'll need another surgery then?" I ask him, my stomach in knots.

"I'm not sure yet. We won't know for a few more weeks. For now, just take it easy. Rest it, ice it if you need to, and I'll write you another prescription for the pain."

I nod, not liking what he's saying but at least it's not like I need another surgery right now. That only adds weeks to my recovery time and I'm already sick of the bandages and slings.

"Thanks, doc."

He nods and I make another appointment for a month from now before I get back in the car and head to Rosewood.

Looks like I'll be hanging around Rosewood for longer than I thought.

FOUR

Evangeline

IT'S the next day and I'm still kicking myself for forgetting about Jasper's father's funeral. I forgot that his dad even lived in town anymore since I never see him around.

I finish arranging the last of the flower pots outside and step back to survey the area. Sydney came by and helped show me the best way to arrange some of the merch and tables so that it looked more organized and pretty.

My back and shoulders hurt from carrying plants and pots around all day but I can't seem to mind the pain when it means that I'm one step closer to achieving my dream.

The sun is starting to set and I know that I should get home and grab something to eat. I finish cleaning up at The Garden Goddess and hop in my truck to head home. Instead of turning right out of the lot though, I turn left.

I find myself headed across town to the Mackelroy's old house. The sun is starting to set and casts a gloomy look over the street. Or maybe that's just how this place looks.

It's on the rougher side of town and I never had much need to come out this way. I pull up behind some car outside of the Mackelroy's house and I'm surprised when I see Jasper head down the steps and toward the car in front of me.

He stops when he spots me and I wave awkwardly as I climb out of my truck,

"Hey," he says joining me in between our cars.

"Hey, how are you doing?" I ask as he leans against the trunk of his car.

His arm is in a sling today and I wonder how he hurt it.

"Good. What are you doing here?" he asks as I shift from foot to foot.

"I just wanted to apologize for what I said yesterday. I didn't really know your dad but it was still a crappy thing to say when you were grieving."

"It's really okay. Gray and I weren't sad to see him gone. We haven't had anything to do with the guy for years."

He doesn't seem too broken up about his dad's funeral and truth be told, if I learned that my father had died, I don't think that I would feel anything either. At least I have my mom still though. Jasper and Gray never really had that either.

"I can see what you mean about needing a land-scaper," I say, changing the subject as I turn to study the old house.

"I think I might need more than that actually."

"For the porch and roof?" I ask, noting the way they sag.

"Yeah, and the rest of the place. I had an inspection done today and I was hoping that I would just have to patch some holes and fix this or that but the whole place has to go. I'm going to have to tear it down and rebuild it or just sell the land."

"Should you be doing all of that remodeling with your arm?" I ask, my eyes straying to the sling.

Jasper laughs, the sound low and husky. It sounds rusty and I wonder when the last time that he laughed was.

"Probably not. My doctor just told me to take it easy until my next checkup and scan, so it looks like I'll need to hire someone to do all of this."

"Well, if you need any help..." I offer and he looks at me with one eyebrow raised.

"Do you know a lot about tearing down houses or building them?"

"Nope, not a thing, actually," I say with a laugh and he chuckles.

"I bet you'd be great at it."

I blush, not used to being praised like that.

"So that means that you'll be in town for longer then, huh?"

"Are you trying to get rid of me?" he jokes but there's a certain light in his eyes that makes me wonder if he's really joking.

"No," I say softly and he grins down at me, his teeth white and standing out against the border of his beard.

"Good."

We stare at each other in silence for a few minutes and I wonder if I should go. My stomach is empty and I want to take a shower, grab something to eat, and then head to bed.

"How's the nursery coming along?" he asks and I smile.

"Great. I can't wait for opening day. I think I have everything set up now. For the most part anyway."

"Good. Let me know if I can help in any way."

"Thanks," I say, shuffling my feet.

"Maybe I can take you out to dinner sometime. We can celebrate."

"Like a date?" I ask, needing to clarify before I get my hopes up.

"Yeah, it's a date," he says with a charming grin.

"Okay," I say and I can feel my cheeks starting to heat with a blush.

"Tomorrow night?" he asks and I nod again.

"I need to work until four or so though."

"That's fine. I'll pick you up at six?"

"Perfect."

Jasper follows me over to the driver's side door and I let him open it for me. His hands go to my full hips and he helps me into the seat. My face feels like it's on fire and I know that I'll be dreaming about his strong hands on me later tonight.

I used to have fantasies about him and those big hands when I was younger. Jasper was the only boy to make me feel like I was on the verge of overheating. He was the only one I ever had a crush on and one of the only people to treat me with kindness.

I was chubby in school too and I can still remember some of the insults or nicknames that the other kids came up with to torment me. Jasper was never like that though. In fact, he was one of the only ones to try to stop it and after a few weeks, it got to be that no one said anything to me when he was around. I used to tell myself that that was why I did everything in my power to have the same classes as him.

"I'll see you tomorrow, Evangeline," he says with a smile and I nod, letting him close my door for me.

He knocks twice on the side as I start the truck up and I wave as I head down the street and back across town toward my house.

Jasper is one of the only people to call me Evangeline instead of my nickname, Evan.

I find that I really like that.

FIVE

Jasper

I'M NERVOUS. I actually changed my outfit three times before I landed on the white button-down and one pair of black dress pants that I own.

It's weird to say, but I'm about to go on my first date and I'm in my late twenties. There just was never any time and no one ever caught my attention. I had enough baggage of my own that I needed to work through before I started bringing other people into my life.

I turn off the road onto Evangeline's driveway. It's long, at least a mile, and by the time I get to the house, my heart is racing with nerves.

Evangeline is outside, bent over some flowers that are growing near the front porch steps and my dress pants start to feel a little tighter as I stare at her perfect peach.

She turns around when she hears my rental car and I smile, parking out front and stepping out to open the passenger door for her.

"You look great," I tell her, and she does.

She's got some deep red dress on that hug those mouth-watering curves perfectly. The high heels give her another inch or two and when she wobbles slightly in them, I know that I need to keep her close and safe.

"Thanks," she says and a piece of her black hair falls out of the bun that it's tied up in.

I reach out, tucking it behind her ear and she blushes, ducking her head and reaching for the seat belt.

I climb back behind the wheel, wondering if I should buy a car soon since I'll be back in the states now and probably staying in Colorado. At least until I hear about my shoulder and find out if I need another surgery.

"Where are we going to dinner?" she asks with that sweet smile that I love.

"Uh, I was thinking about either The Rosebud or Mountain Peak Grill? Is there a different restaurant in town that you like?" I ask her.

I did a search of town and I didn't see any new places that had opened up but I could have missed something or maybe she wants to go out of town to her favorite place.

"No, either place sounds good."

"Which do you like more?"

"I've never been to The Rosebud but I like the grill."

"Want to try The Rosebud?" I ask and she grins at me, letting me know that I made the right choice.

I head back toward town and pull up at The Rosebud. It's an upscale restaurant located on the north side of town. I climb out, waving off the valet so that I can open Evangeline's door myself and she smiles, blushing slightly as I offer her my hand and help her out.

I don't let her hand go as we head inside and up to the

maître d stand. Luckily for us, it's a Tuesday and a little slow so we get seated without a reservation.

The place is done up in varying shades of red with small tables that each have a rose bouquet in the center. Our waitress gives both of us a once-over and smiles flirtatiously at me before giving Evangeline a bit of a dirty look.

My blood starts to boil and I remember how she used to get picked on when we were kids. I had shut that down when I was fifteen, threatening to beat the shit out of anyone who said a bad word to her. From then on, she was left alone.

"Did you want to order some wine or something?" I ask and Evangeline shakes her head.

"No, not for me. I'm a bit of a light weight and I'm afraid one glass and you'll have to carry me out of here."

"I don't mind doing that if you want one," I offer with a smile and she giggles.

"The flowers are pretty," I say, nodding toward the roses.

"I have some at the nursery too," she says as she picks up a menu.

"What's your favorite kind of flower?" I ask as I grab my own menu.

"Oh, I don't think that I could pick," she says with a laugh.

"You like them all, huh?"

"Yeah, it changes a lot. Sometimes it's sunflowers or poppies, sometimes it's dahlias or irises. I guess it just depends on the season or my mood."

I nod, filing that information away for later.

"How's your arm?" she asks after we've both decided on food and have set our menus aside.

"It's okay. A little sore but I iced it and it's better now."

"Good," she says and I can see that she wants to ask what happened but I'm not ready to talk about that yet.

The attack is still too fresh and I luck out when the waitress comes back to take our order. I nod for Evangeline to go first and she grabs her menu, her cheeks pinkening as she tells the waitress her order.

"I'll just have the Caesar salad," she says and I stare at her like she's crazy.

"No, she won't," I blurt out and both women turn to look at me.

"She'll have the steak, medium well with the macaroni and cheese and I'll have the steak, medium rare, with the Caesar salad and baked potato," I order.

Evangeline is staring at me in surprise and I wonder if I did something wrong. I remember how much she liked the macaroni and cheese and burgers at lunch at school and just took a guess.

"Is that alright?" I ask after the waitress has left and Evangeline bites her lip.

"Yeah, I just, I thought that I was supposed to eat a salad on a date."

"According to who?" I ask, outraged at the thought.

"Um, this magazine."

"Well, it's wrong. I want you to eat and be happy around me."

"Then yeah, it's perfect. I love macaroni and cheese," she says with a happy sigh and I smile.

"I remember."

"Really?"

"Yeah, you used to eat it every time that they served it at school. If they weren't serving that, hamburgers, or pizza then you just grabbed something from the vending machine. Usually pretzels and Skittles."

Evangeline looks shocked that I remember that and I take a sip of my water, my eyes locked with hers.

"You caught all of that, huh?"

"Yeah, I caught everything that you did back then," I admit softly.

"Really?" she asks, her eyes filled with excitement and I nod.

"How could I not? You were the most beautiful girl at our school."

"No, I wasn't," she says but she's still smiling.

"Yes, you were. Still are."

The waitress comes back with our food and sets it down a little harder than she needed to and I wonder if she overheard what I said to Evangeline and is pissed.

We dig in and I share some of my baked potato with her. She gives me some of her macaroni and cheese and I smile when I see that she ate it all.

I order us dessert even though we're both stuffed and ask that they be put in a to-go box. The waitress comes back with the dessert and bill and I ignore her flirty smiles as I hand over my card.

She stomps off and I smile at Evangeline.

"I had a lot of fun," I say and she leans forward, resting her elbows on the table, her face in her hands.

"Me too," she says with a smile but I can see that she's getting tired.

"We should do it again."

"Okay," she says as the waitress comes back.

I sign the slip and add the tip before I stand and offer Evangeline my hand as we head back out to the valet stand.

We drive back to her place and I ask her about the nursery and why she never left town.

"I would have thought that you would have left," I admit and she shakes her head.

"I was going to for college at least but then my mom got sick so I stayed here and took care of her."

"How is she doing now?" I ask.

"Better, but she still needs someone to look after her a bit."

I nod, pulling up out front of her house.

"Are you thinking about moving back to Rosewood?" she asks as I shift into park and I shrug my good shoulder.

"I haven't figured out what I want to do next yet," I admit and she nods.

"I hope that you stick around," she says and I grin.

I lean over the seat, cupping her face in my hand and pulling her toward me. Her lips are soft underneath mine and they mold to mine perfectly.

My tongue slides against the seam of her lips and she opens for me tentatively. I slip my tongue inside and we both moan as her tongue moves against mine. Her hands fist in my shirt and I want to feel her hands on me, on every inch of me.

She pulls back and I lick my lips, desperate for another taste of her.

"Have dinner with me tomorrow night?" I whisper against her lips and she nods, then shakes her head.

"I can't, sorry. I have girl's night tomorrow night."

"The night after then," I say and she nods, her nose bumping against mine.

"It's a date," she says with a smile and I lean in, stealing one more kiss.

She climbs out before I can get out and open her door for her and she waves as she jogs up the front porch steps. I watch until she's safely inside before I turn the car around and head back to the hotel.

I need to get my housing and transportation stuff figured out soon. I don't think that I can handle living in this hotel for much longer, but the thought of buying a place here seems so permanent. I'm just not sure that there are many rental places here in Rosewood so I might not have much of a choice.

I'm just about to climb into bed when I remember that I never called Gray to go over the house stuff. I grab my phone, bringing up his number.

I had called Ender, an old military friend who works at Eye Candy Ink with Gray a little bit ago to keep an eye on him and see how he's been doing since the funeral and I hadn't heard from him, so I assumed that everything was fine and that he's handling the loss alright but maybe I should have checked in with him before now.

"Hey, everything alright?" Gray asks as soon as the call connects.

"Yeah, yeah. I'm fine. I was going through the house stuff and well, we should talk about some of it. Are you still at work?"

"No, I'm just headed home now."

"Well, I had the inspection and talked to the realtor and she thinks that we should spend the money to fix the place up before we sell it. Well, first she asked if I was sure that I didn't want to keep it since real estate is such a good investment and this part of Rosewood is really trending up. Do you want the house?"

"Fuck no," Gray hisses out, and I kind of half laugh at his reaction.

"Yeah, I figured."

"Do you?" he asks me, and I snort.

"No. I think we should tear the place down and rebuild though. It might actually be cheaper since Dad didn't keep up on any of it and the roof needs to be replaced along with at least half of the pipes."

I sound old and tired to my own ears and I wonder when I became this person.

There's a beat of silence and I pull the phone away from my ear, wondering if the call dropped or something.

"I'm sorry, Jasper," Gray whispers a moment later and I'm shocked.

"For what?" I ask after a beat and I can hear him swallow.

"For hating you so much for the past seven years. I know that you were just doing what you thought was right, what you thought would be able to provide for us and I've been an asshole. I was so mad at you for leaving me with him."

"I didn't have a choice. Not if we wanted to eat," I say kind of defensively.

The truth is that I've always felt guilty for leaving Gray behind with my dad but I didn't know what else to do.

"I know. I know that, but I still kind of blamed you."

You and me both.

We're silent as those words sink in and I take a deep breath.

"Did you even want to join the military?" he asks.

"It was a job," I say after a minute because the truth is that no, I never really did.

I needed something that was going to pay me enough to live and cover Gray's living costs, and I wasn't able to find that in Rosewood. Everything was too expensive to live in if I went to Denver or Colorado Springs and I still would have been leaving him behind because he never would have left Nora.

"I'm sorry, Jasper," Gray says after a beat.

"It's alright. It's not your fault. You were just a kid."

"So were you."

We are silent as I lie down on the bed and stare up blankly at the ceiling.

"I can come home and help you with the house," he offers.

"You don't have to do that."

"Yeah, I do. It isn't all your problem, Jasper. I'll talk to my boss tomorrow and see when I can take time off."

"Thanks, Gray," I say after a minute and I wonder if he can hear how grateful I am for his forgiveness and help in my tone.

"I'll talk to you soon."

"Yeah," I say and we hang up a minute later.

It feels like I'm finally starting to make some progress with Gray and it's a relief that he doesn't hate me.

My phone rings again and I look at the screen, smiling when I see Brooks' name on the screen.

"Hey man," I say, sitting up on the bed.

"Hey, how's it going?"

"Good, where are you at?" I ask him and he clears his throat.

"I'm in Germany."

"Are you stationed there now?" I ask, frowning.

Brooks was a fellow Ranger, though we were in different teams.

"No, I got shot and blown up so I'm headed back to the states."

"Shit, man."

"I know. I heard the same thing happened to you not too long ago."

"Uh, yeah, a few weeks ago."

"How are you doing?"

"Good, my arm is still banged up but I think the surgeries are done for now. Where in the states are you headed?" I ask him.

If I remember right, Brooks lost his mom when he was twenty so he doesn't have any family left.

"Not sure yet."

"Come to Rosewood. You can help me tear down my dad's house," I say with a laugh.

"Sounds like fun. You got a place there?"

"No, not yet, but I've got a hotel room. I can ask for a different room with two beds?"

"Yeah, sounds good. I'm not sure what I'll do next or how long I'll be there, but it will be cool to catch up together."

"Yeah, let me know your flight info and I'll pick you up," I offer.

He tells me he will and we end the call a minute later.

It sucks that he got hurt, but it will be nice to have a friendly face around here.

My mind flashes back to Evangeline and I smile as I lie down.

Correction. It will be nice to have another friendly face around here.

SIX

Evangeline

I TRY to balance the bottle of margarita mix, bag of tortilla chips, and brownies as I head up the stairs to Rowan's apartment. She lives in town with her little girl, and Sydney and I are headed over for girl's night.

I've known Rowan and Sydney since high school. I was older than them but I was paired with Sydney as part of the senior and freshman mentor program and we hit it off. She was like the little sister that I never had. Rowan and her were already friends so when we hung out, she would join us.

They both left for college a few years ago but Rowan has been back for over a year. She moved back when she found out that she was pregnant and that asshole Reed stopped talking to her. I don't know how you could do that to your pregnant girlfriend and I'm happy that I've never met the guy.

Sydney just moved back and so this is the first girl's

night that we'll have where all three of us are here in a few years and I'm excited to pick up the old tradition.

"Hey, I brought the goodies!" I say as Rowan opens the door and lets me in.

Harper makes a mad dash for the open door and I smile as Rowan leans down and scoops her up.

"Little escape artist," I tease her, poking her nose and Harper giggles.

"She did the same thing when I got here," Sydney says as she reaches out to help me with the groceries.

I set the rest of the food down on the counter and turn to give my friends a hug.

"Sorry for the mess," Rowan apologizes, trying to pick up some of the baby toys and diapers littering the floor.

"Don't worry about it. I'm just glad to be here with you guys," I say, giving her a hug.

"You look great!" Sydney tells her as Rowan pushes some of her red hair out of her eyes.

"I'm a mess," she says with a sigh.

Harper crawls over to me, and I reach down, picking her up in my arms and cradling her against my chest. She reaches up, her tiny little fingers wrapping around a strand of my dark hair. She pulls on the strands, giggling.

"Troublemaker," I whisper against her cheek and she squeals, clapping her hands together.

"Mama, Mama," she calls and I pass her off to Rowan.

"She's probably hungry," Rowan says as she moves to sit down and nurse her.

I join Sydney in the little kitchen, opening up the brownies and tortilla chips. Sydney is already cooking up the ground beef and I move to help her cut up some tomatoes and lettuce.

"She's out," Rowan says as we're plating up the food and I smile.

"Is she sleeping through the night?" I ask.

I'm kind of clueless when it comes to kids. Dating hasn't been on my radar for years, so neither have kids.

"Yeah, she's always been a good sleeper. It's more watching her when she's awake that's the problem," she jokes.

"Nothing that some tacos can't fix," Sydney says with a smile as she hands her a plate and Rowan grins.

"So true."

We all head over to sit down in the living room and Rowan sighs as she kicks her feet up on the coffee table. We dig in, all moaning at the same time and I laugh.

"I've missed this," I say and they both nod.

"What's new around town?" Sydney asks as she dips a chip into the guacamole.

"Not much," I tell her.

"Well, that's not true," Rowan says with a smile. "Word is that a certain someone is back in town."

"Jasper," I say and she grins at me.

"I heard that you went out with him last night."

"Yeah, I did."

"And?" they both ask at the same time.

"And it was perfect," I admit with a blush.

"I knew it! I want all of the details," Sydney says and I laugh.

"Well, we went to The Rosebud for dinner."

"And..." Rowan asks, waiting for more details.

"And the food was really good," I go on.

"You're the worst," Sydney says with a laugh.

"And we kissed when he dropped me off. He said that I

was beautiful and he noticed and remembered all of these things from when we were in high school. It was... perfect."

"Oh my gosh! That is so sweet," Sydney says and Rowan is smiling but it looks a little tense.

I wonder if talking about guys reminds her of Reed and what they could have had.

"What about you?" Rowan asks Sydney. "Any dates or boys that we should know about?"

"Ugh, no. My grandma keeps trying to set me up on blind dates but I've managed to put them off."

"That won't last long," I warn her and she laughs.

"I know, I know," she says with a groan.

"Maybe it will be true love?" Rowan suggests.

Sydney just shrugs and the conversation turns to town gossip. We make virgin margaritas as quietly as possible so that we don't wake Harper.

It's late by the time we call it a night and I walk out with Sydney around midnight.

"It's nice to have you back home," I say, giving Sydney a hug before we part ways and head to our cars.

It was hard not to miss my friends or be jealous of them when they left for college. I never could have afforded it and I used to wonder if I was making a mistake and should have just taken out some loans.

Now it feels like it was meant to be. I'm about to open my own nursery, my dream business, I have a second date with the only man who has ever fueled my fantasies, and both of my best friends are back in town.

Life is pretty perfect right now.

So why does that thought have me wondering when the other shoe is going to drop.

SEVEN

Jasper

"YOU KNOW, most people would wait a day, maybe even two, before asking their guests to do manual labor," Brooks says as he helps me haul out the washing machine.

"You volunteered!" I argue, narrowly avoiding wedging my finger between the washing machine and door.

My shoulder is killing me and I have a feeling that it's going to be sore for a few days after this. Brooks mumbles something that I don't catch and I choose to ignore him as we haul the washing machine out to the waiting truck. Someone from town bought it and the dryer and we're trying to load it before the people from Goodwill come to pick up the couches and end table.

I hired a construction company and they're supposed to come tomorrow to start work on the place. I have to get the place cleared out before then.

"Thanks," Ms. Watson says with a smile as she hands me the cash and Brooks closes the truck bed.

"No problem."

She waves as she heads down the street and I turn back to Brooks. He's rolling his shoulder and I wonder if his shoulder is acting up too.

Brooks got hit in the back and shoulder. He broke two of his ribs and tore a tendon in his shoulder and another in his back near his shoulder blade. Luckily, his ribs are mostly healed by now and his surgery on his shoulder was successful.

"Want me to move anything else? Maybe hop up on the roof?" Brooks jokes and I grin, slapping him on the back.

"Nah, let's take a break and grab a beer."

We head back inside and I open the fridge, taking out the six-pack that I put in there this morning. Brooks twists off his top, taking a long pull on the bottle and I follow suit.

"Nice place," Brooks says carefully as he looks at the dilapidated kitchen and living room.

"Yeah, home sweet home," I mumble.

The carpet is worn and dirty. There are holes in some of the walls and scratches and cigarette burns on most of the furniture. I'd like to say that this was all new but the truth is that it was this bad when I was living here too.

"How are you doing with all of this and your dad?" Brooks asks.

He knows a bit about my family and home life and I'm sure that he knows this is a sensitive subject but I trust Brooks. He's a good guy and I know that he gets it to some extent.

"I'm okay. It's weird being back. When I left, I was like the town pariah and then I went into the military and now people are looking at me like I'm the town's golden boy."

"And that's a bad thing?" he asks.

"Not necessarily. It's just that it feels fake. None of

these people helped me when Gray and I needed it but now they can't wait to shake my hand and welcome me back."

"So, you think you'll be leaving soon?"

"I don't know yet. I'm not sure where else I'd go and I still have my VA appointments here," I say, taking another drink from my beer.

"Is that the only thing keeping you here or does that have anything to do with your date the other night?" he asks with a grin.

"Yep."

Brooks laughs and I drain the last of my beer, pulling out two more for us.

"What's her name?"

"Evangeline. She's a year younger than me but we went to school together and since it's such a small town, everyone knows everyone."

"Is she pretty?"

"Oh yeah. She's got these curves and this pitch-black hair that hangs halfway down her back. She's so sweet and smart."

"Lock that shit down," Brooks advises me.

"I will," I say under my breath but he hears me and grins.

"Let me know when the wedding is."

"You'll be the first invite that we send," I promise.

"How's your brother?"

"I'm not sure. I haven't talked to him in a few days but he seemed alright."

Brooks nods, draining his beer bottle and pointing down the hallway.

"Bathroom?"

"Yeah, first door on the left."

He nods, heading that way and I pull my phone out,

debating if I should call Gray or Ender. I land on Ender and hit dial.

"Hey, Mack. How's it going?" he asks as soon as the call connects and I can hear the buzzing of tattoo machines in the background so I know that he's at work at Eye Candy Ink.

"Hey, pretty good," I say, shifting on my feet.

"I'm sorry to hear about your dad," he says after a beat and I wonder what all Gray has told him about our dad.

"Thanks, that's actually kind of why I'm calling," I start.

"Everything okay?" Ender asks and I can hear the concern in his voice.

"Yeah, I called Gray last night and asked if he wouldn't mind coming back to Rosewood to help me with our dad's house."

"You want me to come with him? I'm not great at construction but I can try," he offers right away.

"No, I'm going to hire a company to help build the house I think. It's more cleaning it out that's the problem right now. I can get it and Gray said that he might come back to help."

"Then what can I do?" Ender asks.

"Keep an eye on Gray for me? We've been talking but things are still a little weird between us and I don't think that he would tell me if something was wrong. You see him every day and I was hoping that you would notice if he was acting strange. Things have been tense for a while with us and we talked about it last night. I just want to make sure that he's okay with everything and is handling the funeral alright."

"I will," he promises and I believe him.

"Thanks, Ender," I say sincerely and we catch up on other things for a few minutes.

I tell him that I'll be in Rosewood at least until I sell the house or land and he offers to show me around Pittsburgh if I'm ever up there for a visit.

Brooks comes back into the kitchen and I say my good-byes to Ender and hang up.

"Was that Gray?"

"No, Ender."

"What's he up to?" he asks and I fill him in.

Special Forces is a pretty small group, and Ender, Brooks, and I have all done a few missions together.

"Pittsburgh, huh?" Brooks asks and I wonder if he'll be headed that way soon too.

"Yeah, he's been there for a few months now."

Brooks nods, picking at the label on his bottle.

"Are you thinking about heading out east?" I ask and he shrugs.

"I'm not sure what to do now. What do I do with my skills and everything that I've learned now that I'm out?"

"Yeah, I've been feeling the same way," I admit quietly.

"I checked out a few veteran meetings."

"How was it?"

He shrugs and I nod.

"I don't think that they can help us pick a career now or anything."

"Yeah, it was more acclimating to civilization now that we're back stateside."

"We could always start a security company?" I offer, only half joking.

"Here in Rosewood? I'm not sure that there would be much demand for it," he says with a grin and I laugh.

"I know. I was thinking of a bigger city."

"It's something to think about. Are you going to want to leave Rosewood though?" he asks and I pause.

A few days ago, my answer would have been hell yes, but now that I've started hanging out with Evangeline, I'm not so eager to leave.

"What time is Goodwill coming?"

"Any minute now," I say, checking my watch.

As if on cue, the doorbell rings and we get back to work, hauling out the last of the furniture and other big items.

"I'm starving. Want to grab something to eat?" Brooks asks.

"Actually, I have to get back to the hotel and change before my date tonight."

"Alright, maybe I'll go out and check out the Rosewood nightlife myself."

"Have fun," I say with a laugh as I climb up into my new Jeep and head back toward our hotel.

EIGHT

Evangeline

"IF YOU DON'T THINK that cookies and cream is the best ice cream flavor, then I think that there must be something wrong with you," I say as we head out of The Little Moo ice cream parlor.

"No way. Vanilla with sprinkles all the way," Jasper says as he takes a lick of his own cone.

"Ugh, so boring," I complain with a laugh as we head down the sidewalk.

"Alright, alright. My favorite flavor is peanut butter ice cream but they were out. Is that better?" he asks as he grabs my hand, interlacing our fingers as we head over to the little park in the town square.

"That's a little bit better," I tease him and he laughs as he takes another lick of his ice cream.

The sun is just starting to set. Jasper picked me up an hour ago and we went to Mountain Peak Grill for dinner before he suggested we get ice cream and take a stroll.

"How was girl's night last night?" he asks as we head down one of the paths that circles around.

"It was good. We had tacos and it was great to catch up. Rowan has a baby girl now. She's seven months old and so cute," I say with a wistful sigh.

"Yeah? Do you want kids someday?" Jasper asks carefully and I realize that maybe I'm coming on a little strong for only our second date.

Everything just feels so easy and natural with Jasper that it's easy to forget that we've only been out twice and are still getting to know each other.

"Yeah, someday," I say with a smile and he squeezes my hand.

"How's the house coming along?" I ask after a minute, trying to change the subject.

"Uh, pretty good. My friend, Brooks, just got to town yesterday morning and he helped me out yesterday with getting rid of most of the furniture. He's going to hang around for a few days or weeks with me."

"I don't remember a Brooks," I say, searching my brain of everyone who went to our high school.

"I met him in the military. He's an Army Ranger too and was injured in an attack overseas a few weeks ago. He's been discharged too and just came for a visit."

"I hope that he's alright."

"He's fine. All healed. Now he just needs to figure out what his next moves are going to be."

"What about you?" I ask him.

"What about me?"

"Are you all healed? Do you have a plan for what to do next?"

Those are the questions that I've been so curious about for the last two days. I don't want to get serious about Jasper if he's going to leave, although I fear that I might be too late on the getting serious part. Which seems crazy because we barely know each other. I mean, this is only our second date.

"I'm healed, for the most part. I might have to have another surgery and until I figure that out, I'll be sticking around. I have enough savings to take it easy until I figure out what I want to do next."

"Well, I'm glad to have you around."

"Good," Jasper says, leaning over and kissing me.

His lips are cold from the ice cream and just as sweet. His beard brushes against me, tickling my sensitive skin, and I smile against his mouth at the feeling. I'm about to wrap my arms around him when I remember that I still have my ice cream cone in my hand.

I pull back before I can smear him with my cone and he laughs, taking my hand in his again. We start to walk again and I smile, enjoying the cool night breeze and feeling Jasper's strong hand wrapped around mine.

We finish the loop in the park and finish off our cones. Jasper wraps his arm around my shoulders as we head back down the street to his new Jeep.

"When did you get this?" I ask him as his car comes into view.

"Yesterday morning. That rental car was getting expensive and it wasn't really my style."

"Now all you need is a new place," I tease him and he laughs.

"I know. That hotel is not ideal, but there aren't a ton of rental properties in the area either. I'm not sure that I want to buy a place here. Not just yet anyway,"

His words have me feeling disappointed, but I guess I shouldn't be. So much of his life is up in the air right now, and buying a house is a big deal. Maybe he's just waiting to hear about his surgery and finish with his father's place.

"Do you like Rosewood?" I ask.

I get the feeling that he's not the biggest fan or why wouldn't he have come back in the ten years since he was gone.

"Yes and no. When I was younger, it was unbearable."

"Why?" I blurt.

"My father, he wasn't... he was an asshole. He was an alcoholic and then a drug addict, heroin I believe. My mother left when we were young because he used to get wasted and smack her around. When she left, he started taking it out on Gray and me."

"Jasper, I had no idea," I say, blinking back tears.

"I don't know that anyone did. If they did know, then they didn't care because nothing was ever done," he says bitterly, and I can understand why he never came back.

"So all of those bruises, they weren't from fights?" I ask.

"Not in the way that everyone thought. I wasn't out starting trouble. I was taking the hits so that he didn't hurt Gray."

"Oh my gosh," I say, choking back a sob.

"It's okay, I'm okay. Gray is okay. When I was eighteen and left, my dad was pretty much gone. I joined the military so that I could send back enough money for Gray to eat and keep the lights on in the house."

"That wasn't your job though. You should have called CPS or the police or someone," I argue, trying to figure out a solution.

"They would have taken him away, he only had a year and a half left in high school. His girl, Nora, was here and he never would have left her."

I look away, my brain racing as I take in all of this new information.

"Nora had her brother Niall here too. He looked out for them while I was away."

Jasper stops walking, turning me in his arms and wiping the tears away.

"Shh, I'm alright. Gray and I are fine," he whispers to me and I nod, trying to get my emotions under control.

So much of what I remember from when we were young suddenly makes sense.

The bruises, how quiet Gray was, how protective Jasper has always been of him.

"I wish that you would have told me. Everyone treated you like you were a menace or a troublemaker. If you told them—"

"If I would have told them, they still would have looked down on me. I would have been that 'asshole Rodney's kid' or that 'poor kid.' Trust me, Evangeline. I've been over this a million times in my head and it sucked, but it worked out. Everyone is healthy and happy now."

I frown, not wanting to let it go, but if he's come to terms with his decisions and is alright with them, then I guess I have to be too. It's not like I can go back in time and change anything anyway.

We reach his Jeep and he helps me into the passenger seat.

"Are you alright?" he asks me, cupping my chin in his hand and tilting my head up until my eyes meet mine.

"I just wish things had been different when you were younger," I admit.

"I know, me too, but they weren't and I can't change that now."

I nod, wiping away a few more stray tears. Jasper leans

in, kissing away where the tears were, and I give him a watery smile.

Jasper kisses my forehead before he steps back and closes the door.

"Want to go anywhere else?" he asks me as he puts the key in the ignition.

"It's so late. I have a feeling that everything is going to be closed in town," I say with a smile.

"Yeah, I didn't realize how much time had passed," he says as he starts the car.

"You know where I always wanted to go?" I ask, thinking back to when I was a teenager.

It seems that I'm not the only one who missed out on stuff when I was growing up.

"Where?" he asks, and I grin as I lean over the console toward him.

"Lookout Point," I whisper in his ear.

"Fuck," he mumbles under his breath as he shifts into drive and heads north toward the famous make-out spot.

We buzz the windows down, letting the cool breeze into the Jeep as we drive up the mountain.

Jasper turns off onto the path that's almost hidden, and we head to the edge of the hill. He turns the headlights off and we stare out at the smattering of lights below us.

"It's beautiful," I whisper.

"Yeah," he whispers back, leaning over the console and cupping my face in his hands.

His lips meet mine and I relax, letting him set the pace. My hands fist in his shirt, tugging him closer to me and we both try to climb over the center console.

His mouth molds against mine, his tongue licking along the seam of my lips until I open for him. He still tastes like vanilla ice cream and it might just be my new favorite flavor.

His beard tickles me and I reach up, my hands cupping his face, feeling the soft strands beneath my fingers. My hands run over the scars there on the left side of his face and I wonder if he minds. He doesn't tense up or anything, too lost in our mouths fusing together.

My hands fall to his shoulders, trying to pull him closer to me. He moans and I pull back.

"Oh my gosh! Your shoulder. I am so sorry," I start.

"Shush," he growls, grabbing me and pulling me back until our mouths meet again.

I let him take the lead, getting lost in the way he tastes, the way that his lips move against mine, the erotic licks of his tongue against mine.

His hands go to my waist and he starts to tug me over the center console. I am fully on board and I move to throw my leg over when my mom's ringtone starts to go off.

"Sorry," I whisper against his lips as I pull back to answer my phone.

"No problem."

"Hello?" I answer.

"Hey, honey," my mom says but there's noise in the background and it doesn't sound like home.

"Hey, what are you doing up so late?"

"Well, I took a tumble. They say I just sprained my arm."

"What? What happened?" I ask and Jasper starts the car, backing out without me having to ask and heading back toward town.

"I fell when I was getting ready for bed. It was just an accident but they won't let me drive home."

"You drove yourself to the hospital?" I ask in shock, but I'm not sure why I'm surprised.

My mom is a tough lady.

"Yeah, it's not that big of a deal. Can you come sign me out?"

"Yeah, I'm on my way. I'll be there in fifteen minutes," I say and she tells the nurse in the room before we hang up.

"Everything alright?" Jasper asks, concerned.

"Yeah, my mom sprained her arm. I need to go check her out and take her home."

We drive the rest of the way to the hospital in silence and he pulls up out front.

"Call me if you need anything," he says as I hop out and nod.

"I'll text you later."

He nods and I close the door, hurrying inside.

It takes me an hour to get my mom checked out and home and in bed. I sigh as I take off my clothes and hop in the shower. My fingers run over my mouth and I remember the way Jasper kissed me tonight. I hadn't wanted him to stop and I'm sure that I still have a red mark from his beard. I wonder how far we would have gone if my mom hadn't called.

I have a feeling that I wouldn't have stopped him from going all of the way.

NINE

Jasper

I SHOW up bright and early, wanting to be the first customer at The Garden Goddess. Today is opening day, and I spent yesterday helping Evangeline out with all of the last minute adjustments that she wanted done.

Evangeline's mom, Marie, was there too. I have a feeling that Evangeline didn't want to leave her alone with her arm, even if she's fine. Her arm is bandaged up like mine and we bonded over tips on how to make the sling comfortable to wear for longer periods of time.

Marie got tired after lunch and had headed to the office to watch some TV show on Evangeline's computer. I had used the privacy to steal as many kisses as I could from Evangeline, but I have a feeling that the beard burn that I was leaving behind may have given us away.

If I moved a pot, she would come over and lean up on her tiptoes, those perfect curves pressing against my body as she offered me her mouth. It got to the point that I was walking around looking for things to do to earn one of those kisses or one of her sweet smiles.

I had wanted to take her out to dinner but I could tell that she was getting tired and wanted to get her mom home to rest, so we made plans to go out tonight to celebrate.

I pull into the lot, parking next to Evangeline's truck. I brought her donuts and a coffee and I smile as I climb out of my Jeep and head inside the nursery.

"Hey!" Evangeline calls, looking over the top of some rose bushes as I walk in.

"Hey, looks great. I brought you some breakfast," I say as I weave through the flowers and plants.

"You're the best," she says as she takes the coffee and takes a large gulp.

Evangeline heads to the front counter and I follow, taking the stool next to her behind the counter.

"Are you ready for the grand opening?" I ask.

"Yeah, I keep checking the clock, waiting for it to be nine."

"Almost there," I say, checking my watch.

"I know, the nerves are killing me."

"It's going to be great," I assure her.

She gives me a grateful smile and I open the pastry box, letting her pick out a donut.

"How's your mom?" I ask as we both bite into our treats.

"Better. She's been icing her arm and resting it for the most part."

"For the most part?" I ask with a laugh.

"Yeah, I keep catching her not wearing the sling. Last night, she kept trying to open this pickle jar. I thought for sure she was going to break her wrist," she says with a sigh and an eye roll.

I laugh. Marie sounds like quite the character. She's

independent, so I don't see her asking for help or taking it easy while her arm heals.

"Hey! Are you open yet?" a pretty brunette-haired girl asks as she pokes her head around the corner.

She looks vaguely familiar, as does the redhead who comes in behind her. The redhead has a baby on her hip and I'm guessing this is Sydney and Rowan.

"Hey, guys!" Evangeline says as she stands to hug them.

"Hey, Harper," Evangeline coos at the baby and I suddenly have a vision of her with our baby on her hip.

I've never really thought about kids or starting a family, but now I can see it, and I want it.

"Sydney, Rowan, you remember Jasper. Jasper, that's Sydney, Rowan, and Harper," she says with a grin as she tickles the baby's side.

"Nice to see you again," I say as they both take me in.

I wonder if I'm up to meeting their standards. Harper giggles, clapping her hands and smiling at me, and I'm guessing that's a good sign. At least that's how I'm going to take it.

"Should we go look at the pretty flowers?" Rowan asks her daughter and she nods her head.

They take off walking among the plants, and I offer Sydney a donut.

"Thanks," she says shyly.

"Want to sit?" I ask, already climbing off of my stool.

"Oh, that's okay," she starts.

"You can have mine. I need to go move those last planters outside," Evangeline says but I wave her off.

"I'll get them for you. Enjoy your breakfast."

I drop a kiss on the top of her head before I head over to where the last of the planters are stacked by the front door and get to work.

"Need me to do anything else?" I ask Evangeline as the first few customers start to come in.

"No, I'm good," she says with a happy smile.

"I've got to head out and meet with the construction crew."

"Okay, I'll see you tonight?"

"Yeah, I'll pick you up for dinner at six and we can celebrate. Anywhere in particular that you want to eat at?" I ask her.

"Can we eat in?"

"Of course. Want me to cook?"

"Can you cook?"

"Oh, yeah. I'm a regular chef," I promise her.

"Okay, Italian?" she requests, and I nod.

"I'll see you tonight. Have a fantastic first day."

She smiles up at me and I lean down, kissing her goodbye before I head out to my Jeep.

I spend the day meeting with the construction crew, grabbing lunch with Brooks before I drop him off at the airport, and then going grocery shopping.

Brooks is heading up to Pittsburgh. He's going to hang out there and see if he likes the big city more than the small town. He's already been in touch with Ender up there and I think he's staying with him for a few days or one of his friends.

"Thanks for the hospitality, bud," Brooks says, hugging me and clapping me on the back.

"Anytime. Don't be a stranger," I tell him.

"I won't. I'll talk to you soon," he says as he grabs his bags and I wave as he heads inside the airport and I hop back into my Jeep.

It was nice having a familiar face around Rosewood and

I'm going to miss rooming with Brooks. Even if he did snore and take too long in the shower.

Evangeline wants Italian for dinner, so I head to the Rosewood Market to grab spaghetti, sauce, and garlic bread.

I changed to a different hotel room and this one has a small kitchen area so that I don't have to eat out for every single meal. It's getting expensive to live there though and I know that I need to make a decision on my future soon.

Five-thirty rolls around and I change into a dark green Henley that reminds me of Evangeline's eyes and a pair of blue jeans before I head over to Evangeline's place. I can't wait to see her and find out how opening day went.

Evangeline is outside on the porch, rocking in one of the chairs there and she jumps up when she sees me, coming over to the Jeep with a smile on her face.

"You look beautiful," I say, leaning over the console to kiss her hello.

"Thanks," she says as she smooths out her sundress.

It's white with red roses all over it and it hugs her chest and flares out at the waist. She's got a white pair of Keds on to match and she looks like a dream.

Like my dream.

I might not know what I want to do with the rest of my life, but I know that I want Evangeline in it.

"How was your day?" I ask her, taking her hand in mine as I drive us back to town.

"It was amazing! Even better than I dared to hope for. I sold a lot and I had a few more requests for landscaping ideas. I think I might have to seriously think about taking up some of these offers."

"You should. You'll be great at it."

"Thanks. The hard part is that I need to hire someone

to cover the nursery while I go out to see the land. I'm not sure that hiring an employee is in my budget right now."

"I can help out," I offer before I can think about it.

"I couldn't ask you to do that," she says as we pull into the hotel parking lot.

"I want to."

I park and get out before she can argue with me some more. She's trying to climb out and I hurry around the hood to help her down before she can dirty her pretty dress.

"Whoa!" she says as I grab her hips and lift her from the passenger seat. "Put me down or you'll hurt yourself."

She's blushing as I hold her above the ground and I grin at her.

"Nah, you're light as a feather," I tell her and she beams at me.

I make a mental note to tell her constantly how beautiful she is and how much I love her curves. I know that kids used to pick on her when she was younger, but I guess that I always thought that she knew that they were just jealous of how pretty she is. I hope that she didn't have any of those thoughts in her head as fact.

"Let's get you upstairs and eat some carbs," I say as I set her down on the sidewalk and interlock our fingers.

We head up to the top floor and I let her into my suite.

"Fancy," Evangeline says as she looks around the place and I laugh.

"Yeah, the fanciest that Rosewood has to offer."

I head past her, spreading my arm out wide.

"So, this is the living room and kitchen area."

"Oh, I like the open concept layout," she says with a laugh.

"Very modern. Over here is the bedroom and bathroom."

She pokes her head into the bedroom, blushing, and I wonder what she was thinking about.

"And that's it," I say as I take two steps over to the kitchen area.

"Very nice."

"Are you hungry?" I ask her and she nods, so I get to work.

Evangeline helps me as I fill a pot with water and preheat the oven for the garlic bread. I open the fridge to ask if she wants wine or something else to drink and that's when I remember the flowers and chocolates that I bought for Evangeline.

"It seems a little silly to get you flowers but I wanted to do something to celebrate your big day," I say as I hand her the flowers and box of chocolates.

"Thank you. I'll never say no to flowers," she says with a wide grin. "Or chocolates."

The water starts to boil and I add the noodles, heating up the sauce and putting the garlic bread into the oven.

I pour us each a glass of wine and start to set the table as Evangeline stirs the spaghetti. We work together in harmony as we drain the spaghetti noodles and pull the garlic bread out of the oven.

I plate the food and Evangeline grabs our wine and leads the way over to the small table in the corner of the room.

"It smells delicious," Evangeline says with a smile as she twirls some spaghetti around her fork.

"Thanks."

We take a few bites and I'm pleased to see that I didn't burn anything or overcook the noodles. We talk while we eat and Evangeline tells me more about the grand opening and her plans for The Garden Goddess's future. She's ambitious and smart, so I have no doubts that she'll achieve all of her goals.

"Can I ask you something?" she asks tentatively and I know before she speaks that it's going to be about how I got hurt.

"Sure."

"What happened to your arm? You just said that you got hurt and they medically discharged you."

I open my mouth but no words come out and I look away.

"If you don't want to talk about it, I understand. I don't mean to pry."

"No, no, it's okay."

I don't want to keep anything from Evangeline, so no matter how much I don't want to go back and revisit that memory, I will for her.

"We were in Afghanistan. Out on a mission. We were supposed to grab a target and bring him back to base to be interrogated."

"I'm guessing it didn't go well," she says softly and I give her a bitter smile.

"No, it didn't. We got there, but the intel was bad. It seemed like the intel was always at least partially wrong, if not total bullshit. We were headed back to the base when we were hit."

Evangeline leans over, resting her hand on mine, her brow furrowed in concern.

"It was an ambush. They hit our Humvees and attacked. I got shot twice but the bigger damage was from a mortar bomb. That's what all of the scars are from. That's what broke my collarbone and there is leftover shrapnel from it that's still in my shoulder."

"I'm so sorry, Jasper. I'm sorry that you had to go through that, to witness that."

"Part of the job," I say, trying to brush it off but Evangeline sees through me.

"Did everyone... did they all survive?" she asks carefully, and I look away sharply, tears stinging the back of my eyes.

"No," I whisper and she's out of her chair and over beside me in an instant.

"I'm sorry," she whispers over and over as I pull her down into my lap and wrap her in my arms.

I let her comfort me as the images from that night play out behind my eyes. I don't want to tell her what it was like watching my friends die, how it felt to not be able to save them, and I don't want those images in her head anyway.

We sit like that until the food is cold and I've pulled myself together. Then she kisses me softly and heads back to her own chair.

I wish that she was back in my lap instantly.

She changes the subject and tells me more about her mom and friends and I listen to her talk as she pulls me out of the darkness that I always go to when I think about that last mission.

"Is that where you got your love of flowers and plants?" I ask as she finishes telling me about her grandpa and the garden that he used to have.

"Oh yeah. He had this big yard with his own greenhouse and he planted vegetables and even had a few berry bushes. They lived over on Planter Street, a few roads away from my mom's place. They passed away two years ago," she says with a sad smile.

"I'm sorry."

"Thanks. I still drive by the place. It's nice to remember them."

"Does someone else live there now?" I ask her and she nods.

"Yeah, I think some family uses it as a vacation place, but they're never really there. At least not that I've seen."

I nod, taking my last bite of garlic bread and Evangeline finishes off her glass of wine.

"That was delicious," Evangeline says as I clear the plates and silverware away.

"Ready for dessert?" I ask and I turn to see Evangeline staring at me with a different kind of hunger in her eyes.

My cock hardens at the look and I swallow hard, dying for something sweeter than the chocolate cream pie that's in the fridge.

TEN

Evangeline

"UH HUH," I murmur, my eyes locked on him.

"Evangeline, we don't have to do anything," he tells me quietly but I shake my head.

I want to. I want to do everything with him.

"Can I see the bedroom again?" I ask, my voice coming out low and husky.

"Whatever you want," he says and I stand, letting him take my hand as we head to the bedroom.

I've never really thought much about when I would lose my virginity. As long as it was with someone who loved me, the other details like where and when, didn't really matter that much to me.

My hands go to the zipper on the side of my sundress and I fiddle with the zipper as I stare at Jasper.

"How's your shoulder?" I ask him as I start to lower the zipper and his eyes shoot up, looking confused for a moment and I giggle.

"It's fine. Can barely feel it," he mumbles as he takes a step toward me, reaching down to help me pull my dress down.

It pools at my feet and I start to feel self-conscious. I'm by no means a small girl, and I wonder if Jasper is going to have second thoughts when he sees me naked.

I don't need to worry though.

Jasper lets out a guttural groan, his hands cupping the back of my head, tangling in my hair and tugging so that he can claim my mouth with his.

"So fucking beautiful. Better than a fucking dream," he whispers against my lips and I blush, pressing my curves closer to his body.

"Your turn," I whisper when he finally lets me come up for air.

He looks uncertain for a moment and I wonder if he's really worried about getting naked in front of me.

He reaches for his shirt, tugging it off and looking away from me as the scars on his left side come into view. This is the first time that I've seen all of them and my stomach cramps at the scars left behind from the attack.

Jasper still hasn't looked at me and I can't stand the thought of him thinking that I'm bothered by them. I lean forward, placing one gentle kiss after another until I've kissed every angry jagged line on his shoulder, chest, and arm.

Jasper looks to me then and I smile up at him.

"So handsome," I say and he grins down at me.

That's all it takes to have him taking control again.

He kisses me, pushing down his pants as my hands go to his shoulders and I cling to him. His body is so hard, so hot against mine and it has me feeling like I'm about to burn up.

Jasper's hands unhook my bra and we pull it off. I'm

way past feeling insecure. As long as he keeps kissing me and touching me, then I'm happy.

His hands cup my breasts, molding the soft globes in his hands and we both moan.

"That feels so good," I breathe as he starts to kiss his way down my neck.

"So perfect," he says back.

He maneuvers me over to the bed and I let him lower me to the mattress. He comes down over me and I spread my legs, aching to feel him inside of me.

His head drops and I watch the top of his dark head as he licks a circle around my areola.

"Please," I beg and he grins but gives me what I need.

His lips wrap around one stiff peak and he sucks it into his mouth. The action has me bowing off of the bed, desperate for him to give me more.

"So responsive," he praises me and I blush, widening my legs. "And so greedy," he teases.

I whine, the sound high pitched as I throw my head back against the pillows.

"Don't worry, Evangeline. I'm going to give you what you need."

His hand drifts over my stomach as he goes back to teasing my nipples. His fingers dip below my panties and I hold my breath as he parts my wet folds and teases that special pearl between my legs.

"Jasper!" I shout as he rolls that bundle of nerves under his thumb and has my legs clamping around his hand and my head thrashing on the pillow.

"Easy," he says against the swell of my breast.

I gasp as he continues to play with my clit, licking and nipping at my breasts. The sensations have me close to the edge and when he presses his middle finger to my tight opening, wiggling his way inside, I go flying.

"Ah! Jasper!" I cry out, my eyes squeezing shut as I come.

"Gorgeous," he says, giving my nipple one last lick before he starts to kiss his way down my body.

He grips my panties at my hips, tugging them down my thighs and I eagerly help him kick them off.

Jasper is kneeling just off the bed and he grabs my thighs, spreading them wide before he buries his head in my wet pussy.

I cry out as his tongue rolls over my clit and my hands go to his hair, tangling in the strands and trying to hold him there. I don't think that there's any need. He doesn't seem to have any intention of moving from between my legs.

He licks up my core, dipping his tongue inside of me and then moving up to circle my little button. He repeats the same path over and over again and it doesn't take me long before I'm right on the edge again.

When Jasper pushes one thick digit inside of me, I come again but he doesn't stop. He fucks me with his finger, stretching me as he continues to lick my clit over and over again.

He prolongs my orgasm and I barely come down when he sends me flying over the edge again.

"Oh my gosh, Jasper," I moan as he kisses the inside of my thigh.

He grins against my skin and I sit up, resting on my elbows to look down at him.

"Is it my turn now?" I ask, my cheeks heating as I think about sucking his cock.

"I need between these pretty thighs."

I shake my head, wanting to pleasure him as much as he just did me.

As soon as he stands, I'm off the bed and kneeling at his feet. His dick is straining at the front of his boxers and there's a few wet spots that have me licking my lips.

I reach up, gripping the soft fabric and pulling down until his cock springs free. He's bigger than I expected and thick. I wonder how I'm going to get him in my mouth, let alone my pussy.

I reach up, wrapping my fingers around his length and the nerves only grow when I realize that my fingers can't even touch around him.

"Evangeline," he starts but I don't want him to try to talk me out of it, so I lean in, opening my mouth as wide as I can over the tip of him.

"Fuck," he hisses out between his teeth and I smile, licking a path up the underside of his cock and tracing the vein there.

My hand wraps around the base of him and I take him in my mouth again, setting up a rhythm with both as I start to suck.

He tastes like man and earth, and I moan at his flavor. His fingers tangle in my hair and I look up at him, my green eyes meeting his bluish-gray.

He looks like he's right on the brink and I suck him harder.

"That's enough! I need you," he growls, reaching down and pulling me up.

He pushes me back down onto the bed and I grin up at him as he reaches down, roughly jerking my legs apart.

He seems to remember himself as he comes down over me and he pauses, looking determined to go slow.

He looks to me as his cock bumps at my opening and I

nod, giving him the go-ahead. He starts to push into me and I try not to wince as he stretches me wide around him.

He goes slow, sinking in one inch at a time and eventually he's fully seated inside of me.

"Fuck," he hisses, dropping his forehead to mine and I smile up at him, running my fingers along his beard.

"I'm okay," I assure him as he studies my face.

He nods, starting to pull out before he thrusts back in.

"Oh!" I moan at the feeling and Jasper closes his eyes like he's in pain.

My fingers dig into his arms and I hold on as he starts to make love to me. At least that's what it feels like and I realize that I'm falling in love with him. Maybe I'm already there. Maybe I never stopped.

My legs wrap around his waist, changing the angle and pushing him deeper, fuller. I gasp and Jasper curses, his pace faltering for a second before he speeds up, starting to pound into me.

"I'm so close," I moan and he nods, sweat coating both of our skins.

His hand grips my leg and pulls it tighter against his side and I raise my hips, meeting each of his thrusts. I can feel his body tightening, tensing against mine and I look up into his eyes.

I could swear that I see love shining there. That look, that's what does it, and I come on his cock, my mouth opening in a silent scream as my release hits me.

He groans, coming with me, and I sag against the bed, letting him move me however he wants.

He rolls us onto our sides, pulling me closer to him to cuddle and I sigh, letting him wrap around me.

"That was good," I say sleepily and he smiles.

"Just good?" he teases and I grin.

"I'm sure that you tried your best."

He laughs, pulling me up onto my hands and knees and kneeling behind me. He enters me slowly and I groan as I feel him fill me up again.

"Let's see if we can do better this time, huh?" he asks me, and I can only nod wordlessly as another orgasm starts to grow inside of me.

I have a feeling that it's going to be a long night. A long and amazing night.

ELEVEN

Jasper

"THANKS FOR COMING DOWN TO HELP," I tell Gray and Nora as we rest, leaning against my Jeep and taking sips from our water bottles.

"Yeah, no problem," Gray says.

He doesn't look super happy to be back in Rosewood but I can't blame him for that. None of his friends are still here and his life is in Pittsburgh now. All that's left for him here are bad memories.

"Did you already get the house figured out?" Nora asks and I nod.

"Yeah, I hired a construction crew and picked out a floor layout. I didn't think that you would care about that."

"I don't," Gray says and I can tell that he's itching to get out of town.

Things have been better this visit. They stayed in the suite next to me and we actually talked about more than our dad's funeral. He told me that he finally asked Nora out and it's been nice seeing them together and so obviously in love.

I told him about Evangeline and my VA appointments and he offered me the guest room in his apartment if I wanted to come for a stay. It's been nice to have my brother back in my life and I'm looking forward to building our relationship more now that I'm back in the states.

"What time is your flight tomorrow?" I ask them as we head back inside to take one last look around the place.

The crew comes tomorrow to start tearing it down and I think it might be cathartic for the three of us to witness it. I asked around town and Nora's dad left a few years ago. Their house sold too and a new family is living there now. The realtor assured me that this area was up and coming so we might be able to make a little bit of money from this sale.

"Are you guys hungry?" I ask as we look around the empty house.

"Yeah, want to grab something to eat on the way back to the hotel?" Gray asks and Nora nods.

We stop at the diner on the way home and grab some takeout and when we get back to the hotel they come over to my room.

"How's your arm?" Gray asks as we crowd around the little kitchen table.

"It's alright," I say as I roll it back.

The truth is that it's been a little stiff and sore lately but it was nothing like when I first got to town.

"When's your next doctor appointment?" he asks.

"On Thursday. They want to do another scan and see how everything healed. If it's alright then I won't need another surgery but if anything has shifted, then I probably will need at least one more surgery."

"And that's on your shoulder?" Nora asks.

"My shoulder and maybe my collarbone."

She nods, worry in her eyes as she looks over my arm and neck.

There are still a few faint scars there but I've been growing out my beard since I got here and they aren't as noticeable now that they're covered.

I remember the way that Evangeline's hands had felt, running over the ones on my chest and arm the other night.

"I hope that you don't need another surgery," Nora says and Gray nods.

"Thanks, me too."

I told them about the accident a few days ago. It was the CliffNotes version but I could still see that Gray felt guilty. We had talked after Nora went to bed and he had cried as I gave him a few more details.

It took me a while to assure him that I didn't blame him for me being over there or what happened and that I didn't regret joining the military to take care of him. I have a feeling that he still blames himself, at least partially, but hopefully over time, we can work past that.

"I'm going to head next door. I want to call and check on the puppies," Nora says and Gray stands, kissing her.

She waves bye to me and I return it.

"How are the puppies?" I ask Gray after she's gone.

"Crazy," Gray says with a smile.

He and Nora adopted two puppies recently, Moose and Marley. They sound like quite the handful from everything that I've heard.

"It's been good hanging out with you," I say, and Gray smiles.

"Yeah, I can't say that I miss Rosewood, but it wasn't as bad being back this time."

"Yeah, I know what you mean. It used to be that everywhere I looked just reminded me of when we were kids, but it hasn't been that way recently," I admit.

"How are you and Evangeline doing?" he asks.

"Really good. She's so sweet and smart."

"I always knew that you had a thing for her," he says.

"Yeah, it seems the Mackelroy brothers weren't exactly great at hiding our feelings for the women that we love."

Gray laughs, leaning back against the couch.

"So, are you staying here? You know I wouldn't mind if you kept the house and wanted to live there. I'm not going to think that you stole from my inheritance or anything."

"Thanks, but truth be told, I don't think that I'm ready for that. It would be like living with ghosts even in the new house."

"Yeah," Gray says, staring up at the ceiling.

We sit in silence for a little bit, both of us lost in our own thoughts. I'm trying to figure out a way to broach a subject that I've been thinking about for a few days.

"I think that I'm going to see a psychologist at the VA or go to group therapy," I blurt out, and Gray looks over at me.

He stares at me for a second before he nods.

"That's probably a good idea for both of us."

"Maybe we can do a few sessions together," I suggest.

Gray nods, chewing on his bottom lip, and I decide not to push it for now.

"Maybe," he says and I nod.

I ask him more about Pittsburgh and Eye Candy Ink. He tells me about Rooney who sounds like either a lunatic or an absolute riot. Harvey is his polar opposite. Then there's Ames and Banks, who both sound to be more relaxed too.

I'm glad that my brother was able to find a second family, one who loves him and is there for him when he needs support. I only wish that we had both had it when we were younger.

I wish that I had it now.

My mind flashes to Evangeline and I smile.

Maybe I already do have someone like that.

TWELVE

Evangeline

"OH, YOU BROUGHT THE GOOD STUFF," Rowan says as she opens the door and sees me standing there with a bakery box from Holy Cannoli.

"Only the best for girl's night," I say with a laugh as she lets me inside the apartment.

"Hey," Sydney says as she comes in behind me, a few pizza boxes balanced on her hand as she tucks her cell phone into her pocket.

"Hey, just in time," I say as I help her make room on the counter for the boxes.

"Where's Harper?" Sydney whispers and Rowan grins at her.

"She's already asleep. She's teething, so she's been crabby today. I gave her some Tylenol and put her to bed early."

"Oh, that sounds rough," Sydney says.

"Yeah, poor baby. I saw some teething toys at the store. They had this cute strawberry one with like a long piece for her to hold on to," I say and Rowan walks over to the sink, pulling out a freshly washed teething toy that I just described.

"I bought it today. Along with some that can be frozen, some numbing gel, some teething pills, and teething biscuits."

"So, you've been busy," Sydney jokes as Rowan sinks onto a stool at the kitchen counter.

"You have no idea."

"We won't stay long then," I promise her, and she gives me a grateful smile.

We all dig into the pizza and take seats in the living room.

"How's The Garden Goddess?" Rowan asks and I nod.

"Really good. Business has been pretty steady since I opened. I had a few more landscaping requests today."

"Are you going to start offering that service?" Sydney asks and I shrug.

"I'd like to, but I need to find someone to cover the shop then. Jasper said that he would help, but I can't pay anyone right now and I don't know..." I trail off.

"Well, you don't have to decide tonight," Rowan says kindly.

"Yeah, what she said," Sydney says with a grin.

I finish off my first slice of pizza and the topic changes to Sydney's job hunt and Rowan's photography business.

"How are things going with you and Jasper?" Sydney asks as we clean up our dishes.

"Um, pretty good," I hedge but they catch on to my hesitation.

"What's going on? You guys seemed so good at the grand opening," Sydney says and Rowan nods.

"They are. I don't know. I think that I'm in love with him."

"You are in love with him," Sydney says and I huff out a laugh.

"I know," I admit.

"So, what's the problem then? He seems just as into you as you are in him," Rowan says.

"I'm not sure that he's staying in Rosewood. He, uh, he had a really rough childhood here. I don't want to get into details because they aren't mine to share, but let's just say that I can't blame him for not wanting to stick around."

Sydney and Rowan can both read between the lines and they blink back tears, sharing surprised and sorrowful looks.

"I don't want to get too attached to him if he's going to leave soon," I explain.

"You don't think that he would stay to be with you?" Sydney asks and I shrug.

"Would you want to leave to be with him?" Rowan asks.

"I don't know. I just opened my nursery here, my mom is here, and I grew up here. This place is my home and I don't really want to leave."

They nod and Rowan heads to the kitchen to grab the bakery box.

"Maybe he'll surprise you," Sydney suggests but I'm not sure.

I don't really blame him for not liking it here, but it seems like a bad reason to end a relationship because I don't want to leave this small town.

Jasper is the only man that I've ever been interested in and he's damn near perfect. He supports me, makes me feel stronger, constantly tells me how beautiful and amazing I am. He protected me from bullies when I was younger and kept an eye on me, all while dealing with his shitty home life and keeping his brother safe.

Is it selfish of me to ask him to stay in this town with me if it's only going to remind him of his childhood and cause him pain? If the roles were reversed, I know that he wouldn't hesitate to leave with me.

"You need to talk to him," Sydney says gently and I know that she's right.

"Yeah, you're going to spin yourself in circles until you can figure this out. Talk this out with Jasper and then you guys can make a plan to move forward."

I nod. I know that they're right. Now I just need to work up the courage to have that conversation.

Part of me wants to bury my head in the sand. Things are good right now. Why should I rock the boat?

Rowan nods and she looks like she's about to fall asleep on her feet. Being a single mom has to be exhausting and I know that we should let her get some sleep.

"Why don't you let me watch Harper tomorrow," I suggest. "You can sleep in or take a bath or something and I'll take her into the nursery with me."

"Are you sure?" Rowan asks, looking grateful and I nod.

"I can pick her up and hang out at the nursery too," Sydney says and we make a plan to have her pick up Harper and come hang out at The Garden Goddess for a few hours.

"Thanks, guys," Rowan says and we hug her goodbye before we head downstairs.

"I'll see you tomorrow," Sydney says and I wave as I head over to my truck.

The streets are deserted and it doesn't take me long to

make it home. I change and get ready for bed but I can't seem to fall asleep.

There's a niggling feeling in my gut. One that's telling me that everything is about to go wrong.

THIRTEEN

Jasper

I'VE BEEN busy with the contractor at the old house, but that hasn't stopped me from noticing that Evangeline seems to be pulling back from me, from this relationship.

At first, I figured that it was just her worried or busy with the new business and her mom, but it's been a few days now and she's still doing it.

It's starting to drive me crazy.

I have my doctor appointment tomorrow and I'm feeling good about it. With the house finally torn down and them getting started on building the new one, it feels like things are finally starting to fall into place.

Now I just need to find out what's going on with Evangeline.

I know that she's still at work, so I head over to The Garden Goddess. It's almost closing time and I'm hoping that I can catch her before she heads home.

There's only one other car in the lot when I pull up out

front and they look to be loading up, so I assume that they're leaving.

I park my Jeep next to Evangeline's truck and hop out. She's starting to haul in some of the planters by the front door and I step over to help her.

"Hey," she says, sounding surprised to see me there.

"Hey, how's it going?"

"Good, pretty good."

She seems nervous and I wonder what I did to make her react that way.

"Is everything okay?" I ask.

"Yeah," she says too quickly.

"Evangeline, what's going on?" I ask as I set the planter down inside the shop.

She won't look at me, just keeps shifting from foot to foot and my stomach drops. What the hell could I have done to get her to act like this.

"Hey, you have to tell me what I did wrong so that I can fix it," I tell her gently, cupping her face in my hands.

"I... I need to talk to you about something."

"Anything," I say right away.

"I'm never leaving Rosewood."

"Okay—" I start, wondering where this is coming from but she cuts me off.

"My mom is here and I just started this place," she says, her hands waving around the nursery as tears start to form in her eyes.

"I know that."

"I... I just, I understand if you want to leave. I know that you need to figure out what you want to do with your life and where you want to live and that you might want to be closer to your brother or..." she rambles on and I blink, wondering what brought all of this on.

"I told you that I hadn't made any decisions yet on what I wanted to do with the future. Where is all of this coming from?"

She looks away, brushing at the tears that have escaped and are sliding down her cheeks.

"I need to protect myself. I need to protect my heart," she says quietly.

"From me?" I ask her and she still won't meet my eyes.

"You can hurt me, you know? I just don't want to get even more attached to you if you're going to leave soon."

I open my mouth, intending to reassure her that I'm not going anywhere, but can I really do that?

Rosewood hasn't been that bad since I've been back, but do I really want to live here for the rest of my life? There's a lot of places in the world, a lot of places with no memories or baggage for me.

"Jasper, do you want to stay in Rosewood?"

She studies my face and I rack my brain. I can't help but think about Gray. I would like to be closer to him and living near him would probably help with that. Do I want to live in a big city though? What would I do for work? I guess I could hook back up with Brooks and we could figure something out, the security business we talked about.

I stare down at Evangeline and I want to tell her that I'm staying, that I want to be with her too but I just can't. I need to figure out my next moves before I promise Evangeline anything.

Evangeline's green eyes are swimming in tears and it breaks my heart to see her this way.

"Evangeline," I start, but she backs up, spinning on her heel, her black hair flying behind her, and hurrying out the doors.

I watch helplessly as she climbs into her truck and pulls out of the lot.

I want to go after her but it feels like maybe we both need some time to think about things.

Could we just not be compatible?

I know that I love her. She's the only one that I've felt this way about and I don't want to lose her, but can I be happy here in Rosewood? Can I really forget everything that happened to me in this town?

Maybe things will be better after the house is finished and sold. Maybe a few therapy sessions and I'll be able to handle the feelings that this town has me feeling.

Unfortunately, I won't know any of that for a while and I'm not sure that Evangeline will accept that answer.

I finish bringing in the planters and I turn off the lights, making sure that everything is closed down before I lock the front doors and head over to my Jeep.

I climb in and head back to the hotel, riding the elevator up alone. As I enter my room, a feeling of loneliness hits me. It's the same way that I used to feel when I was younger. Strange that the emotion is only hitting me again now that things are up in the air with Evangeline.

I head to the bedroom, lying down on the mattress that has been killing my back for the last few weeks and I wonder if maybe it is time to finally pull myself together and figure out what I want to do with my life.

And who I want to do it with.

FOURTEEN

Evangeline

I STARE BLANKLY out the front windows of The Garden Goddess, watching as the rain pours down. It's been raining all week which has seriously hurt business, but I don't mind. The weather seems to fit with my mood.

It's been a week since Jasper and I talked and I left here in tears. I haven't seen or heard from him since. In fact, I heard that Jasper isn't even in town anymore. Word is that he packed up, checked out of the hotel and headed to Pittsburgh.

Part of me is happy to hear that he's getting to spend some time reconnecting with his brother. He is the last bit of family that Jasper has left, but I still wish that he had chosen me.

I miss him.

I turn away from the window, walking around the nursery and checking that all of the plants have enough water. I've already done it twice today and it's a lousy way to distract myself.

My phone goes off and I can't help but hope that it's Jasper.

It's not.

SYDNEY: **We're worried about you, Evan!**
Rowan: Yeah, we're here if you want to talk.

I KNOW that they want to help me through this, but I don't think that they can. There's no amount of margaritas, tacos, or brownies that can fix the hole in my chest.

EVANGELINE: **I'm fine. I promise. I'm just going to need some time.**
Rowan: You missed girl's night.
Evangeline: I know, I'll be there next week. I promise.
Sydney: We're here if you need anything before then. You can always call an emergency girl's night. You know that we'll be there.

I SLIP my phone back in my purse and sigh as I turn to stare out the windows again. It's still coming down hard out there and I wonder if I should just close up for the day and head home. I can make some soup and grilled cheese and join my mom as she watches her soap operas this afternoon.

I'm about to start turning off the lights and locking up when a familiar black Jeep pulls into the lot.

My stomach drops and my heart starts to race. I'm not sure how to react to the sight of Jasper climbing out into the rain.

Our eyes lock through the front windows and he gives me a slight, hopeful smile as he heads through the rain to the door.

"Hey," he says as he reaches up, shaking out the water from his dark hair.

"What are you doing here?" I blurt out and his hopeful look drops.

"I wanted to see you. I need to talk to you."

"About what?" I ask, crossing my arms over my chest.

"I missed you," he says.

My resolve starts to melt at his words but I remember the way he left town without a goodbye and I straighten my shoulders.

"How's Gray? I heard that you went to Pittsburgh," I say, trying to remain civil.

"He's good. He and Nora are engaged."

"Congratulations! Is that why you went up to see him?"

"It was part of the reason. I found out that he was going to propose and wanted to be there to help them celebrate."

"What was the other reason?" I ask.

"Um, therapy."

"What?"

My arms drop as I stare at him in shock.

"I went to do a joint therapy session with Gray. He's been seeing someone up there to talk about our dad and everything that happened when we were kids."

"Wow, um, how was it?"

That doesn't feel like the appropriate question to ask here, but I'm not good at this.

"It was good. Kind of eye opening. It was interesting to see what Gray remembered compared to what I remembered. He, uh, he told me more about what it was like to live with our father after I had enlisted."

I step forward, reaching out and resting my hand on his arm.

"I guess I'm lucky that Rod just stopped going home. It probably would have been worse for Gray if he was there with him, but I don't love the fact that a sixteen, seventeen-year-old was left alone for weeks or months on end. If I wasn't sending back money..." he trails off and my mind pictures a scared and helpless Gray at sixteen, all alone in that old house.

"I'm sorry, Jasper."

"I know. Me too. We talked more, went to two sessions together. The work is far from over, but it's a step."

"Are you moving to Pittsburgh then?" I ask, swallowing hard.

"No. I heard back from the VA doctor and I don't need a new surgery. I do know that I need help dealing with the accident and some other stuff that happened overseas, along with my childhood shit."

"So, you're going to the VA then?"

"Yeah. I'm going to a group veteran session and then I made an appointment for one-on-one too."

"Good, I'm glad that you're getting help," I tell him honestly.

"I'm messed up, Evangeline. I have these moments where I feel like I'm going to break out of my skin. I don't want to go back to that house and seeing it tore down made me feel like crying," he says, his voice breaking.

Seeing him like that smashes my heart into itty bitty pieces and I want to cry too.

"I'm so sorry, Jasper."

He nods, looking down and swallowing hard.

"I know that you think that I want to leave Rosewood, and that's partly true, but if this week without you taught me anything, it's that I need you. I was miserable without you."

"Wouldn't it be better for you if you left Rosewood though?" I ask, afraid to get my hopes up.

"I don't want to leave you. I felt even more alone when I was in Pittsburgh and I don't want to be in a big town. I want to be with you."

"Are you sure?"

"Yes. I'm so sure that I bought a house here."

He reaches into his back pocket, pulling out some papers and handing them over to me. I scan them, my mouth dropping open as I reread the lines.

"You're buying my grandparents' house?" I ask, my eyes filling with tears.

"Yeah. I put in an offer and it was accepted two days ago. I still have to close on it, but I'm staying in Rosewood."

I look down at the papers, my heart beating out of control in my chest.

"I know how much their house meant to you, how much you missed it. I'd love it if you would eventually move in with me. I know that we're moving fast, but I love you. I only want to be with you, Evangeline."

"I love you too," I say, wrapping my arms around his neck and burying my face in his chest.

He wraps his hands around me right away, holding me tight against him, and I cry happy tears.

"I only want you. I don't care where I live as long as I'm with you. We can make better memories here together. I love you," he whispers against the top of my head and I squeeze him tighter.

"We will," I promise.

We stay like that for a long while, just holding each other and enjoying being back with each other. It's still raining, so Jasper helps me lock up before he drives me back to the hotel.

He helps me out of my wet clothes and my body starts to heat as he pulls off his own. I know that we have a lot to talk about, but right now I just want the man I love to make love to me.

Jasper seems to be on the same page and he steps forward, cupping the back of my head as he bends down to kiss me. His lips meet mine and I melt against him, letting him take the lead.

We pull off the rest of our wet clothes and he picks me up, carrying me into the bedroom and spreading me out on the bed. He makes love to me slow that night, the sweat mingling with our wet hair and skin and helping us move together.

We come together and I smile up into his eyes.

"I love you," I whisper, my hand running up his shoulder and over his scars.

"I love you too," he says, kissing me as he pulls out and rolls onto his side.

"I'm glad that you came back," I tell him, rolling onto my side to face him.

"There's nowhere that I would rather be."

We spend the rest of the night making love and plans for the future. He tells me more about therapy and I know that he has a lot of work to do to be fully okay with Rose-wood, his childhood, and the accident, but I'm happy to be by his side while he works through everything.

There's nowhere that I would rather be.

FIFTEEN

Jasper

"I'LL WATCH HIM," Marie offers, reaching out with a smile.

"You're going to hang out with Grandma, alright Noah?" I ask my two-year-old son and he nods, reaching out to go to Marie.

I smile as I go in search of my wife. We're in Pittsburgh, visiting Gray and Nora for Thanksgiving and we invited Marie to join us. She loves Gray and Nora and they love her. She's like the mom that none of us ever had.

Moose and Marley look up from their dog beds as I head past them, so I bend down, scratching their ears. They've calmed down a lot over the years and they're easier to manage now that they're out of the puppy phase and don't chew on my shoes every time I come to visit. Noah loves them and I know that Evangeline is going to be wanting a dog when we get back home. I've already started researching breeds because what my Evangeline wants, I make sure that she gets.

"Hey, how are you feeling?" I ask Evangeline as I come up behind her, wrapping my arms around her swollen stomach.

"I'm a whale," she says, getting a little teary-eyed and I bury my face in her neck to hide my smile.

Evangeline is seven months pregnant with our second baby, a girl this time. We've been married for four years, got engaged on our one-year anniversary. She moved in with me at her grandparents' place six months before that, and I knew that I wanted to spend my life with her.

"You're beautiful," I promise her. "Every inch of you is perfect."

I rub her stomach, kissing her neck as I try to reassure her. I'm used to the baby hormones by now and I'm an expert at calming her worries. It doesn't hurt that she still is the most beautiful thing that I've ever seen, so telling her isn't any hardship.

"Are you hungry?" I ask her as she turns in my arms.

"Always."

I smile at her, kissing her before I lead her over to the couch next to her mom.

"I'll go grab you something to eat," I tell her and she smiles up at me before she reaches for Noah.

I head into the kitchen where Nora is busying feeding her son Sawyer.

"Hey, little man," I say, holding out my hand for a high five.

He grins at me as he slaps it.

"Gray should be home any minute and we can get started making the sides," Nora tells me and I nod.

"I was going to grab Evangeline some of those veggies and dip."

"Help yourself," she says with a smile.

I make Evangeline a small plate and am cleaning up the kitchen when Gray comes back in with a few grocery bags.

"Going to the store on Thanksgiving is a nightmare," he says with a sigh as he kisses his wife.

"No sh— crap," I finish, looking over to make sure that Sawyer didn't hear me.

Gray elbows me and I give him an apologetic smile but he just grins at me.

The two of us are closer than ever. We both went to therapy for a few years and I would sit in on his session every couple of months. It was the right thing for us. We both worked through our childhood and residual feelings for our parents.

Hearing him talk about what it was like when I left for the military was hard to hear and there were a few sessions where he just yelled at me and got out all of the emotions that he felt when he was left alone.

We've moved past that though and Gray left therapy a few months ago. I'm still going and still attending the veteran group meetings. I've come a long way from when I was first discharged.

"What can I help you with?" I ask Gray as he starts lining up ingredients on the counter.

"Want to make the green bean casserole?"

"Sure."

I take my spot next to him at the counter and get to work. The turkey is almost done, so now we need to make the sides. Gray gets to work on the mashed potatoes, occasionally stopping to kiss his wife or hang out with his son.

We've been taking turns with holidays for the past few years although usually we come up to Pittsburgh. Gray and Nora have the dogs here, but they also have more family here.

I've been working at The Garden Goddess, running the place so that Evangeline can do landscaping jobs and focus on the growing part of the business. We've grown the place over the last five years and now we have people from Denver and Colorado Springs coming to buy my wife's flowers.

"What time is everyone else getting here?" I ask Gray and he checks his phone.

"Should be any minu—"

"The party has arrived!" Rooney calls as he opens the front door and I laugh.

"They're here," Gray says straight-faced.

The townhouse fills up fast and I laugh as I dodge kids and everyone else to make it back to my wife and son.

"I grabbed you a roll," I whisper to her, passing one to Marie and Noah too.

"My hero," she says as she takes a big bite and I laugh.

She's right though. I want to be her hero, the love of her life.

Her everything.

"Love you," I say as my hand goes to her belly, rubbing her baby bump.

"I love you too. So much."

I steal one more kiss before Ender is calling me over to the kitchen. If you had told me five years ago that I would be happily living in Rosewood, working at my wife's greenhouse and nursery, and in therapy, I probably would have laughed in your face.

I'm glad that it's my life though.

Ender passes me a beer and Brooks comes over to join us, his arm around his wife, Rae. It's been nice to see all of my old military friends happy and settled and I'm glad that we all stayed in touch.

"Time to eat!" Harvey calls and I grab Noah so that Marie and Evangeline can get situated first.

"Happy Thanksgiving," Ender tells me and I smile, clinking my beer bottle against his as I go to join my family.

ABOUT THE AUTHOR

CONNECT WITH ME!

If you enjoyed this story, please consider leaving a review on Amazon or any other reader site or blog that you like. Don't forget to recommend it to your other reader friends.

If you want to chat with me, please consider joining my VIP list or connecting with me on one of my Social Media platforms. I love talking with each of my readers.